Rage at the Devil

When stable hand Ben Cade returns home to visit his father, he is stunned to discover the old farmer has been killed by drinking poisoned whiskey. Suspicion falls on a peddler who has recently passed through the Nebraska town of Gothenburg asking strange questions, allegedly to locate old friends. Ben has vengeance in his heart, but his shooting ability is woefully lacking.

A chance meeting with Wild Bill Hickok, his boyhood hero in dime novels, sees the legendary gunfighter teaching him the rudiments of his dubious profession. Ben proves to be an able student. A new confidence finds him setting out on a merciless quest for retribution. But the fortuitous acquisition of a gun-toting reputation brings dangers he could never have imagined. Will Ben have the maturity and wisdom to meet the unforeseen challenges fate throws in his path?

Rage at the Devil

Dale Graham

A Black Horse Western

ROBERT HALE

© Dale Graham 2019
First published in Great Britain 2019

ISBN 978-0-7198-3031-0

The Crowood Press
The Stable Block
Crowood Lane
Ramsbury
Marlborough
Wiltshire SN8 2HR

www.bhwesterns.com

Robert Hale is an imprint
of The Crowood Press

Typeset by
Derek Doyle & Associates, Shaw Heath
Printed and bound in Great Britain by
4Bind Ltd, Stevenage, SG1 2XT

ONE

OLD NICK CALLS
THE SHOTS

Dark clouds hovered menacingly over the small Nebraska cemetery located on a wind-swept hillock one mile exactly outside the town of Gothenburg. The golden orb had doffed its hat and retired as if in communion with the sad occasion taking place below. After all, this was not the time to be enjoying the warmth and pleasure of a bright sunlit morning in early June. Quite the opposite in fact.

An impressive gathering had assembled around the open grave following the committal service in the local church. Jacob Cade was, or had been, a popular figure in the Platte Valley. Especially when he had new-laid eggs to sell. All that had ended when his body was discovered by his son, Ben. The boy had abandoned the life of a dirt farmer, preferring to tend horses in one of the local livery stables.

The town was the first major stopping off point on the Oregon Trail for the wagon trains after leaving Omaha in the eastern part of the state. Here they could rest up and obtain supplies and fresh horses before continuing their three-month trek to the Willamette Valley in distant Oregon. The constant flow of settlers seeking a new life on the west coast provided a good living for those employed in Gothenburg's horse trading business.

It was on his weekly visit to the homestead that Ben's life was turned upside down. The youngest son of Jacob and the late Molly Cade, Ben was the only member of the family present at the funeral. His elder brother had failed to show up. That was easy to explain away.

Solomon Cade had left the family smallholding the previous year. Like many other adventure-seekers Sol had been lured away by the prospect of untold riches from the latest gold strike in South Dakota. Nobody knew where he was now. The last message had been a scrawled letter telling the family he had reached Deadwood and was assessing his prospects. That had been six months before. There had been no further communication since.

A line of meadowlarks perched on grave stones were listening avidly to the stilted rendition of a suitably funereal hymn. Their feathers rippled beneath the stiff breeze gusting in off the level prairie lands appropriately named Dismal Flats. The wind struggled to snatch away the preacher's strident tenor vocals. As the final refrain faded, everybody bowed their heads, the preacher opening his prayer book ready to deliver the final eulogy.

His black gown flapped around thin legs giving him the appearance of a manic raven. Nobody laughed as the sonorous dirge was intoned. 'Let us now commend the body of our brother Jacob to the mercy of God.' He paused to take a handful of earth held in a box by a young acolyte, sprinkling it onto the cheap pine box. Slowly, the bearers began lowering the coffin into its final resting place. 'And so we therefore commit his body to the ground, earth to earth, ashes to ashes, dust to dust, in the sure and certain hope of a resurrection to eternal life.'

Sobs followed from the more emotive members of the congregation as the procession to offer a similar token of respect began. Each participant whispered a few words of sympathy to the young man standing alone on the edge of the grave. Ben accepted the platitudes with a brief nod. Even amidst all his father's friends, he still felt isolated and a tad uncomfortable with all eyes fixed on his response to this bleak occasion. Having to wear his Sunday suit and black shoes that pinched his toes did not help. He was far more comfortable in dungarees and a slouch hat with a hay fork clutched in his hand instead of a Bible.

Ben's eyes were fastened onto the mound of soil clattering onto the coffin lid. Along with the expected grief and torment, a bubbling hostility was evident in the stiff tight-lipped posture. Although he

7

tried to maintain a sorrowful woebegone expression, anger was evident in the narrowed gaze. Teeth were clenched tight, bunched fists informing the observant watcher that the boy had reprisal and revenge in his heart.

For the death of his father was no accident. Ben could have more easily accepted a termination caused by the old man falling off his horse and breaking his neck, or some other unfortunate mishap. It was the nature of his passing that tore at the lad's heart. Once again recalling the terrible discovery in all its grim and sordid detail made Ben see red.

It was on his last visit home as he approached the soddie that Ben knew instinctively something was amiss. The hens, usually corralled in their own pen, were running wild. And old Blue, the family bloodhound, was howling a mournful lament outside his kennel. What in thunderation could have happened?

Ben called out. But there was no answering response. The place seemed deserted. 'You there, Pa?' he called out, suspecting the worst. Jacob Cade would never have left his holding unattended like this. Ben leapt off his horse and hurried inside the cabin, to be met by the awful truth. His father lay sprawled across the floor. A howl of unrestrained anguish issued from the boy's open maw.

A cursory examination revealed that Jacob was clearly dead. The blood drained from his son's face. There was no sign of any injury caused by a struggle. Had the old-timer suffered a heart attack? Then his gaze shifted to the table, where a bottle of liquor had been upended. And there another shock awaited the distraught young man. The house cat employed for its skill in catching mice lay just as dead, having jumped onto the table and lapped up the spilled contents of a whiskey bottle.

That was when the awful truth dawned. The hard fact was impossible to ignore. Both man and beast had been killed by poisoned hooch. He grabbed up the bottle and read the name printed on the label – The *Devil's Revenge*, finest five-star whiskey – contaminated rot gut more like. In a rage of fury, he threw the bottle at the wall, where it smashed in a welter of glass fragments. Ben staggered outside and flopped down on the stoop. His brain was whirling around in a ferment of chaotic emotions trying to figure out what had happened.

Only when he had simmered down and boiled up a pot of coffee was he able to think straight. After mulling over the stark facts, he arrived at the sobering conclusion that some passing drummer must have sold the poor dupe bad liquor. Since his wife had passed away the previous year, taken by a bout of cholera, Jacob had begun drinking more. Whether this particular session had been by accident or design made no difference to the distraught man. Ben had only one thought now in mind. The *Devil* who had perpetrated this heinous crime would be hunted down and it would *Cade's Revenge* that exacted an appropriate justice.

The haunting refrain of the twittering mead-owlarks brought the distraught young man back to the present. The cemetery had emptied. The gravediggers had completed their grim task, leaving Ben alone staring down at the mound of earth below which his father now lay. One other man had, however, stayed behind. Town marshal Pake Addison had noticed the simmering rage burning beneath the surface and knew in which direction the stricken youngster's thoughts were leaning.

He laid a cautionary hand on Ben's shoulder. 'Best to leave this to the authorities, Ben,' he intoned quietly. 'I've already sent a letter to the county sheriff's office in North Platte. He'll organize a posse to go after the culprit.'

Ben shook off the consoling gesture. He had little faith in the actions of a faceless bureaucrat a week's ride away. And the marshal was of little use, his jurisdiction ending at the town limits. No. Ben knew his only hope was to track down the seller of the lethal *Devil's Revenge* and deal with the skunk himself.

Yet all he did was nod, allegedly accepting the lawman's advice. 'Guess you're right, Pake,' he muttered. 'No sense taking the law into my own hands.' Satisfied, the marshal patted the boy's shoulder. 'That's the only way for justice to be gained,' Addison concurred. 'Vigilante law is no way for the state to move forward.' Believing that he had made his point, the lawman left.

'But that's exactly what I aim to do,' Ben mumbled under his breath. 'I'll make sure the rat who did this pays the full price, Pa. You can bet on it.'

Over the next few days, Ben arranged for the

holding to be looked after by a neighbouring farmer, making him promise not to let the marshal in on his plans. 'You certain this is a wise decision?' his pal Chalkie White counselled. 'You ain't no gunslinger, Ben. And this guy could be dangerous.'

'What choice do I have?' he replied. 'That old soak of a sheriff in North Platte has no idea what he's looking for. And I've been practising with my six-shooter. I'll track him down alright. Flat Nose George, the bartender at the Snake Eyes saloon, told me a whiskey drummer passed through the week Pa was killed. And he'd been asking some odd questions.' He paused to gather his thoughts. 'The critter said he was trying to locate old friends he'd teamed up with to work a gold claim at Pike's Peak back in 1858.'

'What's so important about that?' his bemused friend asked. 'It's a long time ago. Must be all of. . . .' The young sodbuster stroked his chin as he struggled to work out the numbers.

Ben helped him out. 'It's sixteen years. Too long far as I'm concerned. Who searches out old associates after all that time?'

'Maybe he just wanted to resurrect the old days over a few drinks,' Chalkie suggested, instantly regretting the foolish insinuation as it struck home.

'Yeh, old buddy. And see what happened,' Ben mocked scathingly, although he held no grudge against his pal for the unfortunate blunder. Hurrying on, he added, 'Pa told me he was at Pike's Peak in that particular year before he realized prospecting

11

was all work with little reward. Only the lucky few struck it rich.' Ben's eyes narrowed. 'He also said he'd been threatened by claim jumpers. Him dying like ain't no darned accident.'

'You figure this guy has some kind of crazy beef against those same thieves,' Chalkie suggested. 'Maybe they stole his poke, then left him for dead?'

'That's exactly what I reckon,' Ben eagerly agreed. 'George said he seemed like a regular drummer when he called at the Snake Eyes. He even bought two cases of this *Devil's Revenge*, which has been well received by his customers.'

'Sounds mighty strange to me,' Chalkie said scratching his head. 'The guy must have a screw loose.'

Ben nodded his wholehearted agreement. 'I reckon he's got two kinds of whiskey, one for regular sales and the other stuff to further this blind vendetta he's embarked on. The maniac has set his sights on rubbing out anyone who was at Pike's Peak in that year – guilty or innocent.'

Ben drew his pistol and twirled it around his middle finger. The slick manoeuvre had been learned from a dime magazine. Called the Denver Roll, it drew a gasp of admiration from his pal. He finished with the Border Shift before nonchalantly returning the gun to its holster. 'Like you said, the guy has clearly lost his marbles. Well I aim to scotch his game permanently. Other poor saps must have suffered the same fate as Pa. And there are likely others in his sights. The murdering critter has to be stopped.'

The two friends parted, Ben leaving with Chalkie's good wishes for success in his mission. 'You take care, old pal,' he advised as Ben mounted up. 'This guy is obviously a fanatic who'll stop at nothing to achieve his madcap ambition. I only hope your shooting skill is as good as those tricks.' But the manic gleam in Ben Cade's eyes indicated he was not listening. He had the bit between his teeth and only the blood of his adversary would assuage his own lustful yearning.

TWO

LESSON FROM A LEGEND

The avenger was eager to get started on his mission. The only clue he had as to which direction the killer had taken was a final gem of information the rat had let slip to Flat Nose George. The drummer's next call was north to Broken Bow in Custer County, so that was where Ben would head.

But first he needed to get in some practice with his revolver. It was a second-hand .36 Navy Colt with a polished bone handle engraved with a horse's head. Ben had saved up for a whole year before buying the much-prized weapon. The only difficulty was that he had made little progress in emulating the skilful dexterity of his hero Wild Bill Hickok, whose stories he avidly consumed in the monthly dime novels passed around from farm to farm.

14

Wild Bill favoured the Navy, of which he had a matching pair. Nobody around here had ever set eyes on the man himself whose reputation was legendary. All that was known for certain about his current whereabouts was that he had taken up marshalling in the Kansas cow town of Abilene.

An hour had passed since Ben had begun his shooting practice. And already over half his stock of lead shot had been fired off with little sign of any progress. Being able to hit a standing target was proving far more difficult than he had expected. Two hits out of ten was bad news, and only then when he had slowed his draw sufficiently to take aim. He shuddered to think about taking on a moving target.

Perhaps he should have been concentrating on this aspect of gunplay rather than perfecting those showy tricks that had so impressed Chalkie White. Deadly Dan Dupree had thwarted his opponents in the latest comic strip with dexterity that had been described in detail at the end of the story.

Dazzle friend and foe alike with these mind-boggling techniques, all guaranteed to mystify opponents and give you the edge in any gun battle – the advert had promised. No mention had been made of the vital need for shooting practice. Ben scoffed at his gullibility. While boasters were busy displaying the 'shift, roll and pinwheel', an opponent would have stood back and calmly plugged you in the gut.

The warning from his pal regarding the adverse nature of his manual dexterity now came back to haunt him. What use were fancy manoeuvres without accuracy of shooting? The raucous blast of gunfire had scared off the usual array of wildlife that frequented the environs of the Cade farm hoping to snap up any discarded scraps.

Only the ever-loyal Blue remained, immune to his master's inept display of marksmanship. The dog wandered across to offer some much-needed commiseration. Ben gave the bloodhound an affectionate stroke. Nevertheless, the boy did not lack determination and resilience. There was too much at stake for him to give up now.

He was out back of the cabin starring angrily at the line of tin mugs perched jauntily on a fence. They appeared to be laughing at his futile attempts to dislodge them. His teeth ground angrily. 'You critters ain't gonna beat me,' he shouted out once again, dragging the gun from its holster.

But he never got to fire the next shot.

A deep-throated northern burr interrupted the action. 'You'll be lucky to hit a barn door at ten paces shooting like that.' The young farmer swung around, his mouth hanging open like a hooked trout. A ruddy flush suffused his stubble-coated cheeks at having his ineffectual efforts being witnessed. This guy must have been watching him for some time.

The newcomer sitting astride a coal-black stallion peered down at the younger man. A half-smile split the rather shallow face made even wider by the flat white plainsman that he always favoured. 'Although I'm glad to see you've had the good sense to buy a Navy Colt. All we need to do now is teach you how to use it.'

But what stunned the boy into immobility was the rippling moustache and goatee beard. Enhanced by long straggly locks of golden brown hair cascading over his broad shoulders, the newcomer was even wearing that trademark buckskin jacket. Ben could only stand and stare. It couldn't be. Surely there had to be some mistake. Yet there he was in the flesh, flashing those blue eyes and actually speaking to Ben Cade. And didn't he look the same as in those De Witt ten cent romances.

Wild Bill Hickok no less!

Still Ben remained stiff and rigid as a poker. 'Ain't you gonna invite a passing stranger to step down and water his horse?' the newcomer said quietly with the hint of a smile gracing the angular features. 'Me and Shadow here have been on the trail since sun-up. And we're plumb tuckered out.' The pack mule trailing behind on a long halter indicated that the surprise visitor had ridden far.

Realizing this was no dream he was having, Ben snapped out of his reverie. 'S-sure th-thing, Mister Hickok sir,' he stammered out, snatching the hat from his head and bowing. 'The creek's over yonder. When you're done, come inside and I'll fix you up with some chow.' The boy's face had lit up knowing he was actually talking to the renowned gunfighter.

'No need to treat me like some pompous dignitary, son,' the tall man averred. 'Plain old Bill will do just fine.'

Inside the cabin, with his revered guest settled and enjoying the promised refreshment, Ben quickly dug out the magazines that had so captured his imagination. 'Jeepers, young fella,' the object of his idolization declared with a hearty chuckle as he thumbed through the garish revelations. 'I ain't never seen these before. They sure build me up into some kind of superman. When it comes down to it though, I'm just an ordinary guy trying to make an honest living. But some fellas just won't let me be. So I get a mite peeved when they cause me bother.' That was a whimsical yet blatant understatement of the true facts regarding the gunfighter's lurid history.

Ben was all eyes and ears. Sitting here chewing the cud with the famous frontiersman was a dream come true. What would his pals say when they found out? 'How did you come by your nickname?' he asked of his quietly spoken guest. Hickok's demeanour just didn't seem to fit the image of the gun-toting hardcase he had expected. This fella was softly spoken and amiable.

Hickok thought for a moment. 'I came into this world as James Butler hailing from Troy Grove, Illinois, way back in 1837. And that name stuck until 1861 just after the War had broken out. I hired on as a lowly stable hand to a mean-hearted cuss named Dave McCanles.' The big man scowled at the recollection of his ill treatment under the freight owner's control. 'On account of my somewhat handsome bearing' – he paused, laughing at himself as he jabbed a finger at the curved nose and short chin – 'the skunk never let me forget it and began calling me Duck Bill. He certainly lived to regret it. Though

I can assure you, young fella, shooting that critter was in self-defence. And that's what the court decided by acquitting me.'

Ben eagerly nodded his concurrence with the verdict. The august visitor then went on to describe the event that had later helped carve his legendary reputation out in stone as Wild Bill. Hickok was visiting a friend who owned a saloon in Independence, Missouri. A bunch of roughnecks came in and started a brawl because they weren't being served fast enough. 'I get plumb annoyed when folks forget their manners,' he intoned firmly. 'Ain't no call for it.'

When the troublemakers began throwing bottles around Hickok hauled out his twin Navy Colts. He punched a hole in the ceiling to gain their attention. Then he proceeded to hustle them outside onto the street. Thoroughly cowed by the bold and decisive action, not to mention a couple of sore heads from Hickok's gun barrel, the disconsolate group were herded out of town. The townsfolk cheered the daring exploit, one woman calling out – 'Good for you, Wild Bill!'

'And it stuck. Been following me around like a bad smell ever since.' Bill sighed, while enjoying a third slice of pecan pie. 'Trouble is with a sobriquet like that, you inevitably have to live up to it.' He shrugged as if the impediment had caused him no problems. Indeed, if truth be told, he relished the attention.

'So what brings you to these parts?' Ben asked, now thoroughly at ease in the great man's presence.

19

'Just passing through on my way west to South Dakota. I hear tell there's another big gold strike in Deadwood Gulch. Aim to make me some dough at the tables by relieving those miners of their poke.' Wild Bill lit up a cigar, offering one to his host and then lighting it as well. Both men drew on the fine Havanas, content in each other's company.

It was Ben who resumed the conversation. 'My brother is somewhere up there. I might join him once I've attended to some erm . . . unfinished business that needs my attention down here.'

Bill shook his head. 'Hard rock mining is a mug's game unless you strike it rich. Take my advice, boy and make your pile selling them guys the essentials of life. In my case it's the pleasure they get from gambling.' He shrugged. 'Sometimes I'm a loser, but most times I'm smiling all the way to the bank.'

Ben was listening avidly, but he still wanted to hear more about this legend's exciting life. 'I heard you were working as town marshal in Abilene,' Ben enquired. 'What happened to make you leave?'

'I took over from Bear River Tom Smith,' Bill narrated, taking a long swig of the lemonade. He was quite happy to talk about his past exploits. 'I was hired for my shooting ability, unlike Tom who let his fists do the talking. Unfortunately the poor guy paid for his bravado with a coward's bullet. Problem was, I became too good at my job. By the end of 1871, they didn't need a gun-toting lawman anymore.'

'That was some years ago,' Ben remarked. 'What you been doing since?'

'After the town council dispensed with my services, I joined Buffalo Bill on one his show tours around the eastern cities. But it was all make-believe play acting. I hankered after the real thing. After drifting around some, I heard about the gold strike and so here I am.' He sat back willing to bask in this young pretender's admiration. 'So why are you so eager to improve your shooting skills, Ben? I'm figuring that your *unfinished business* must have something to do with it.'

The younger man's faced clouded over. He remained tight-lipped. 'Must be something perty doggone bad,' Bill espoused with sympathy. 'Maybe I can help you out with my particular area of expertise.'

Slowly, with measured deliberation, he was able to tease out the macabre course of events that had led to Jacob Cade's untimely death. 'I had a similar occurrence happen to me in Abilene when a sneaky rat sold bad rot gut from a wagon before heading back east to Topeka. I caught up with the skunk outside Junction City and burned his whole stock to the ground. I would have sat the guy on top of the wagon but he objected. So I just shot him instead.'

The admission was delivered in a nonchalant manner as if he had merely just given the victim a scolding. Ben was mesmerized. All the perilous deeds described by Wild Bill did not fit the man sitting opposite. Yet it was clear as daylight that the affable persona could change at the drop of a hat to be replaced by the cold-blooded killing machine described in the lurid novels flooding the territory.

21

Ben's guest then stood up. 'I'm obliged to you for such fine vittles,' he complimented his host. 'It sure has picked me up. Where in tarnation did you learn to cook like that?'

'Ma taught me the rudiments,' Ben replied with pride. 'She always said that a good cook would always be in demand.'

'She sure wasn't wrong there. A wise woman.' Hickok smiled as he finished the delicious lemonade and popped the last cookie into his mouth. 'But time is money as they say. So we best be getting outside to give you some vital lessons in effective gunplay before I hit the trail.'

They stepped outside and Bill watched his protégé display the skill or lack of it that he had been practising hard to perfect. After the fourth bullet had failed to hit the target line of tin cans, the instructor called a halt to the ineffective action. 'You're doing it all wrong,' he told the impatient novice. 'This is how it should be done.' In the blink of an eye the twin Colts stuck in Hickok's belt were palmed and spitting hot lead. All four mugs disappeared from the fence.

Ben was struck dumb by the virtuoso performance. Eyes bulging, mouth agape, all he could do was stand and stare. Finally he found his voice, croaking out a despairing bleat of failure. 'I'm never gonna be as good as that.' He threw down the pistol. 'What's the use in even trying?'

Bill patted him on the shoulder. 'Don't do yourself down, boy. We all have to learn the hard way. Best

22

that you had me come along to point you in the right direction. Now pick up that Navy and let's turn you into a proper gun handler.'

Over the next two hours, Wild Bill ironed out all the faults that had been holding his student back. Chief among them was the way Ben snatched at the pistol in his belt holster. 'Speed is all well and good when you're as experienced a gun hand as me. Most important though is not to rush your shooting. Too many fellows reckon speed equals accuracy.' He wagged a finger of dissent. 'It ain't so. They're the ones who usually end up cooling their heels on Boot Hill. Take the time to aim properly and always for the guts. Not an easy task when you're facing down a target that shoots back. It might not be a killing shot but the shock paralyses the victim's brain, giving you time for the final take down.'

More good advice followed, such as standing side on to offer a reduced target. And wearing a pistol with butt inward for a cross draw. 'Faster and more accurate in my humble opinion,' was the studied verdict. 'And I'm still here as proof it works.'

Old Blue sat outside his kennel watching the two humans blasting away at tin cans. He shook his noble head, bemused by the strange ways of these bipeds. Other creatures had cautiously returned to view the bizarre side show, sensing that they were not the target of the shootists. Squirrels, rabbits and even a wandering coyote sat perched on rocks as if the presence of this celebrated trigger expert had passed down the animal grapevine.

By the end of the session, Ben was still only hitting half the mugs, but it was a distinct improvement, alongside the modification of his stance and bearing. 'Practice makes perfect is a very good saying,' Bill advised, slotting the Navy Colts back into his waistband. 'And remember what I said about challenging another gunman. You'll need to develop nerves of steel so as not to panic and fumble the draw. That's gonna be the hard part. Anybody can knock hell out of tin mugs. But facing down another human being takes pluck and a sturdy backbone.'

Before the famous visitor mounted up he reached into his saddle-bag, removed a bone-handled Navy and handed to his protégé. 'I've always found that two are better than one. Makes you learn to shoot with both hands. That can be a very valuable asset.'

Ben was too stunned to offer his thanks. They shook hands. Eventually he did mange to blurt out his appreciation of the generous gift. 'I don't know how to thank you, Bill.' Ben's heartfelt indebtedness brought a tear to his eye. 'I'd most likely have ended up eating dirt if'n you hadn't moseyed on by.'

'Glad to have been of help,' the gunfighter said. 'Perhaps we'll meet up again some day and you can regale me with your own tales of derring-do.' He waved a hand, nudging his horse towards the north. Ben stood watching until his celebrated visitor had disappeared. Then he sat down on the stoop twiddling Blue's ears, wondering if the last few hours had actually occurred.

Or was it all just a dream?

24

THREE

HELLFIRE AND DAMNATION

Chalkie White was not due to take over until the following morning, which gave Ben plenty of time to ensure all the animals were fed and watered. Then he saddled up and tied his bedroll behind the cantle. There was no knowing how long his search for the killer would take, so he packed enough trail rations in his saddle-bags for a week. Anything beyond that and he would need to reconsider his situation.

Conviction of an early overhaul of his quarry was evident in the beaming expression. His unexpected encounter with Wild Bill had boosted Ben's confidence considerably. After the celebrated gunfighter had left, Ben had resumed his target practice with renewed vigour, enacting the useful skills his benefactor had taught. By the time his ammunition was

25

finished, he was hitting eight out of ten cans, a substantial improvement.

The need to replenish his ammo meant a detour to Gothenburg. He entered the town a different man from the one who had left to bury his father. Gone was the woebegone stoop, in its place was a broad-shouldered, manly bearing. He exchanged his mustang for the best horse in his stock, namely a fine chestnut mare. The holster had been abandoned, with the two revolvers stuck into his waistband, butts inwards for the cross draw. Ben Cade had learned his lessons well.

His first call was to the livery stable to inform the owner that he had been called away to tend a sick relative in Wellfleet and would be absent for a week. It was a small town exactly opposite to the direction he intended travelling. Barney Duke hummed and hawed, but could not rightly prevent such a compassionate mission. Ben felt guilty about having to deceive him.

Unfortunately there was no other choice. Barney was a likeable enough jasper, but even the local members of the Women's Temperance League had expressed shock when news of his gossiping nature burned their twitching ears. The guy just couldn't keep his mouth shut. Divulge his true intentions and Marshal Addison would know about it before he'd even managed to obtain fresh lead shot and spare cylinders, as advised by Wild Bill.

Keeping a low profile, Ben was soon heading out of Gothenburg in the southerly direction expected.

Only when he was beyond the curiosity of prying eyes did he alter course for his true destination. After crossing the rickety bridge spanning the Platte River, he followed the south bank of the broad sweep, weaving a tortuous path through stands of dwarf willow. The next accessible crossing point was by the Cozad ferry, ten miles downstream. From there Broken Bow was a straight trek due north across the rolling grass-clad landscape of the Great Plains.

Only the occasional homestead was passed, where Ben was able to split the breeze with sodbusters eager for news of the outside world. Their homes were built almost exclusively of cut earth, trees being in short supply except along the river banks. On each visit he casually made enquiries as to whether a man answering to the description handed down by Flat Nose George had called. Luck favoured his enquiries at the last soddie visited, where the nester recognized the description.

'Strange kinda guy,' the farmer remarked, scratching his head while topping up Ben's coffee mug. 'Not often you come across fellas wearing a brown and yellow check suit and sporting a grey Derby. A drummer if'n ever I saw one. And sure enough, I was proved right when he tried selling me some firewater called *Devil's Revenge*.' Ben allowed the farmer to ramble on, knowing that he was on the right trail. He knew how lonesome it could get stuck out on the plains with only your dog for company. 'He kept asking if'n I'd done any prospecting around Pike's Peak. Now what in Hades is that all about?'

Ben sure could have enlightened him, but he held his peace. The farmer's very presence told him the answer had to be in the negative.

'He a friend of your'n?' the man asked. Not wishing to broadcast his true reason for the enquiry, Ben brushed off the question by claiming the man owed him money. He left soon after eager to play catch up.

Broken Bow was another booming township catering to the needs of homesteaders heading west to start a new life on the vast open spaces. The newcomer was hoping that his quarry would have decided to lay up here for a spell. Straight away he nudged his horse through the amalgam of wagons over to the nearest saloon on the far side of the busy street.

The Arrow Head proved to be a lucky choice. Even before he made enquiries from the bartender, the bottles of *Devil's Revenge* lined up on the rear counter caused his heart to skip a beat. Clearly this was the good stuff. Ben ordered a slug, cautiously sipping the amber nectar.

'Jeepers bartender, this stuff packs a mighty wallop,' he was able to confirm. 'The guy who made it sure got the name right.' That said there was no denying it was a top-quality product. He struggled to conceal the anger bubbling away inside his lean frame. Again proof indeed that this dirty chiseller was living a double life hawking two conspicuous brands of the same product. Further tentative probing revealed the double-dealing drummer's name was Deacon Crabbe and he had taken a room at the National Hotel across the street.

Only ten minutes in Broken Bow and he had run the skunk to earth. Not wishing to appear too inquisitive, he changed the subject, lingering over his drink before nonchalantly exiting the saloon and making a beeline for the hotel. There was no supply wagon outside the National, which indicated Crabbe was parked behind.

Traversing the thoroughfare churned up by ox-drawn wagons was a dicey task requiring agile dexterity. Safely across to the far side Ben, slipped down a passage adjoining the hotel. And there was the sales wagon, large as life and twice as deadly. A pair of lop-eared mules still in the traces indicated the skunk must be on the verge of pulling out.

A rear-access stairway built as a safeguard against the ever-present threat of fire gave access to the upper storey. Ben kept watch for any sign that the drummer was ready to leave Broken Bow. Ten minutes passed slowly and he was growing impatient. All set to boldly mount the steps and confront the rat in his room, Crabbe suddenly emerged onto the veranda.

In the nick of time, Ben leapt back into the shadows as the drummer descended clutching a valise. Clearly he was ready to leave. The plan was formed to make his presence known somewhere on the trail where there would be no chance of the local law intervening.

Ben followed his quarry at a respectable distance,

ensuring he could not be spotted. Only when the wagon pulled off the trail into a copse of trees to make camp did he make the decision that the time for retribution was at hand. Knowing the moment had arrived, he could feel his heart racing, hammering inside his chest. The cogent advice of Wild Bill helped calm his nerves. *When you draw that gun it becomes an extension of your arm; never haul iron unless you're prepared to shoot.* The advice of the renowned gunfighter was clearly embedded on his mind.

A few deep breaths, a flexing of the fingers, and Ben Cade was ready. He tied up his horse and cautiously approached the drummer's camp. The smell of frying bacon made him realize he hadn't eaten all day. It was also a homing beacon of where his quarry was innocently ensconced. A grim smile played across the young hunter's face. But no humour reached his cogent gaze, only a fervent need for reprisal. He paused at the edge of an open glade watching his quarry, whose whole being was focused on the preparation of his evening meal.

Ben was fixated with the notion that it would be the killer's final chore. But first he decided to play the skunk just like he would a hungry trout. 'Hallo the camp!' he called out, making his presence know. 'Any chance of a wandering traveller sharing your vittles?' Anyone riding into a camp unannounced was likely to receive a bullet rather than the expected hospitality indicative of the frontier.

'Come right in, stranger,' came back the chirpy reply. 'I can always throw on another slice. And there's plenty of beans.'

Ben approached the drummer, studying him carefully for any surreptitious moves. Crabbe was around the same age as old Jacob and sported a grey moustache. Hard eyes beneath beetling brows peered back at the newcomer. 'Sit down, mister, and help yourself to some coffee. It's strong and black. You heading far?'

The crunch question! Ben carefully considered his words before replying. He took a sip of the hot liquid, continuing to study the garishly clad killer. He decided to play it cool and enjoy the proffered meal before shattering the skunk's self-assurance. 'Just heading where the mood takes me,' he remarked, forking a piece of bacon into his mouth. 'And yourself?' he asked casually.

'Reckon I'll head for the Platte River,' Crabbe replied. 'I'm a whiskey drummer. There's plenty of settlers passing through who'll appreciate the good stuff.' Ben could barely contain his anger at this blatant distortion of the truth. But his face remained deadpan, expressionless.

Only after some more inane trail chatter did Ben choose to posit an unsettling change of tack. 'Actually, I'm heading for Pike's Peak where my pa made his fortune before losing it all at the tables.' A slight stiffening of Crabbe's shoulders, a widening of the cold gaze, told Ben this piece of information had struck a nerve. 'I'm hoping to pan enough gold for me to pay off the bank loan on our farm.'

Crabbe leaned forward. 'I was down there back

'58. Maybe I knew your pa.' The drummer's fist had turned white as he clenched the fork poking at the bacon.

'Could be,' Ben responded calmly, leaning forward to emphasize his follow-up remark. 'Only trouble is, he was killed recently by some drifter passing through Gothenburg.'

Beads of sweat bubbled up on Crabbe's brow, his coarse features turning a noxious shade of grey. He stood up. 'I'm sorry to hear that, mister.' His voice held a tremor of edginess as he moved across to the wagon. Reaching inside, he removed a bottle that Ben couldn't fail to recognize as *Devil's Revenge*. He flipped off the cork and made to tip a hefty slug into Ben's coffee mug. 'You look like you could benefit from Deacon Crabbe's special elixir for raising jaded spirits.'

A hand shot out covering the mug as Ben gave a baleful reply. 'I've sworn off the hard stuff, Mister Crabbe. It didn't do my pa much good either. But don't let me stop you enjoying your own creation.' Ben slowly rose to his feet. 'In fact I insist on it. Let's drink a toast to past friends. Me with this coffee and you with that marvellous whiskey.'

'Don't reckon I'm in the mood for a drink neither,' was the stuttered response.

'That's not very obliging. What kind of drummer refuses his own goods?' It was a question that required no answer. A cutting edge had hardened Ben's tone. 'I'd say it's the type who plies bad whiskey to prospectors who were at Pike's Peak back in July of

32

1858. Just like you did to my pa.' The tightness around the mouth had replaced a blasé smile. 'Now you drink that rat poison and let's prove that it's the good stuff as you claim.'

Crabbe backed off. 'I don't know what you're talking about, mister. You've gotten the wrong guy. My whiskey is top class. I just don't feel like any at the moment.' His eyes twitched nervously.

The Navy Colt had jumped into Ben's hand. 'You're a damned liar.' The hammer snapped back. 'You drink that or so help me I'll drill you where you stand.' Anger, hate, disgust transformed the handsome visage into a merciless purveyor of unfettered retribution.

'You can't shoot an unarmed man, mister,' the drummer whined raising his hands. 'It ain't right. That would be cold-blooded murder.'

Ben considered the plea for mercy. 'Guess you're right there. I should rightly take you in to stand trial.' He shook his head at that notion. 'But then some smart-ass lawyer would likely get you off on a technicality. That's no answer. So I'm giving you the chance to walk away.'

One of the Colts was removed from his belt and carefully placed on the log where Crabbe had been sitting, the other being slotted back into his waistband. 'All you have to do is lean across. I'll even give you an edge.' Ben placed both his hands behind his head. 'Can't say fairer than that, can I?'

The sly drummer was considering his options as his right hand crawled towards the waiting six-shooter.

Ben watched his every move, judging when the action would blow up. Hickok had told him to study his adversary for any hint betraying that he was ready to make his move. Unfortunately he had failed to point out that too many scheming braggarts didn't play by the rules.

Deacon Crabbe was one such low-life. All of Ben's attention was focused on the hand stretching towards the revolver. He failed to heed that in his other hand the brigand still held a full mug of hot coffee. No warning was given as he suddenly tossed the contents at Ben's exposed face.

'Aaaaaaaagh!' The cry elicited was more from surprise than pain. Lucky for him, the hot liquid splashed across his raised arm, thankfully encased in a thick flannel shirt. But the devious tactic caused him to stagger back as Crabbe lunged for the proffered pistol.

The villain howled with triumph, braying like a demented mule. 'All of them thieving claim jumpers deserved to get the *Devil's Revenge*.' He managed to snap off a single shot. But it was poorly aimed due to Ben having tripped over the guy's saddle. Whistling past his head, the bullet had fatal results for an unfortunate prairie dog caught in the line of fire.

The younger man quickly recovered his wits, palming the belted Navy and returning fire. Once, twice, three times the revolver spat flame; the grim reaper finally able to make his presence felt with the fourth ball. Crabbe screamed as his windpipe disintegrated, blood pouring from the puncture wound.

The final two shots emptied the chamber. Ben was taking no chances. Both struck dead centre, heart shots that effectively terminated any chance of a resurrection.

Deacon Crabbe, fixated purveyor of liquid death in the form of *Devil's Revenge*, had been stopped in his tracks. No more innocent prospectors would suffer at the hands of this fanatical avenger. Standing over the dead man, Ben's heart took some time before slowly returning to its normal steady beat. His hand still clutched the empty pistol, smoke twining from the barrel.

His face was white, eyes bloodshot staring down at the corpse. There was no getting around the fact that terminating your first human being is apt to leave a man in shock. Wild Bill had been right in that respect. It was the squealing of a prairie dog grieving over its lost mate that jerked Ben out of his reverie. The truth that his bitter quest had been completed in such ruthless fashion meant it would take some time for his traumatized brain to steady.

To avoid any repercussions for his resorting to vigilante justice, he would need to get rid of the body. Ben hustled across to the wagon and pulled aside the cover, revealing numerous cases of the fiery tipple. Feverish delving among the stock brought a ghoulishly satisfying cackle to the young man's lips. He had found the one case containing the poisoned hooch clearly marked with a red cross.

There was only one way to deal with this. But he would need to locate a far more secluded place for what he had in mind. Tethering his horse behind the hooch wagon, Ben slapped leather and moved deeper into the remote terrain removed from the main trail.

An hour later he came upon a track worn down by what appeared to be cattle hoofs. Ben had given up hope of finding a remote enough spot for that day when the unexpected gash in the soaring cliff wall offered a favourable site. Here was a box canyon in which to enact a fitting tribute to the heinous skulduggery perpetrated by Deacon Crabbe over the years.

The only bugbear was whether it was still in regular use. He gingerly urged the horse-drawn wagon forward. A mile inside the enclosed canyon he came across a corral long since abandoned. The man's face crinkled in satisfaction at the isolation, a knowing smile forming at the sight of a discarded running iron. This had clearly been a hideout for a gang of cattle thieves. A fleeting notion as to the fate of the rustlers was forgotten as Ben set about putting his own surreptitious scheme into practice.

After releasing the horse from its traces, Ben manhandled the body of the deceased drummer onto the top of the crates of liquor. This was gonna be like a New Year's Eve celebration. A pile of kindling placed below the wagon was set alight. Assisted by some tallow fat found inside the wagon, the whole caboodle was soon well ablaze.

Ben stood well back all set to enjoy the party accompanied by a bottle of the good stuff. The rest were soon popping and exploding as glass shattered in the intense heat. The watcher couldn't resist whooping with glee, waving his arms around. 'Ain't you enjoying this up there, Pa?' he hollered out, fully caught up in the exhilaration of the moment. 'Just look at the darned critter, perched there atop his own funeral pyre. He sure got the message. Anybody who messes with the Cades picks up a deadly pay-check.' He tipped the bottle to his lips and slurped a hefty slug of the powerful liquor.

Sometime during the night he was jerked awake. Sweat was pouring down his face, his heart pumping in hysterical abandon. A harsh cry of terror issued from the open mouth. 'Keep away! Keep away!' he yelled out. Arms flapped wildly, desperate to ward off the awful vision of the burning drummer shuffling towards him. His staring eyes blinked wide in petri-fied terror.

Ben gasped and shuddered, his tormented brain reaching the conclusion that it was all a hideous nightmare, interrupted by a wandering coyote sniff-ing around the camp. The animal ran off, equally fearful of this demented figure. Never was he more glad to be awake than at that moment. He lay down allowing the manic tattoo of his heart to return to normal. What was left of the night passed without any further disturbance, but it would take some time before the full horror of the bizarre funeral faded from his mind.

FOUR

THE LAUGHING JACKDAW

Only the cawing of a vulture managed to bring Ben out of the arms of Morpheus the next morning. The empty bottle close by told its own tale. He groaned aloud, head pounding following the overindulgence of Devil's Revenge. The sun was already high in the sky. Sensing a meal in the offing, scavengers had edged closer to the supine form sprawled some distance from the burnt-out wagon. Smoke drifted up from the charred skeleton, writhing like an incensed rattler.

The sudden wrench from his drunken lethargy scared the predators off as Ben lurched to his feet. His mouth tasted like a rotten slab of bacon. He coughed, staggering over to a handy creek to douse his splitting head with cold water. Hard liquor rarely touched his lips. Ben Cade much preferred a foaming glass of beer any day. But with all that hooch going spare, and his nemesis stoking up the fires of Hell, he had felt justified in celebrating the success of his mission.

But never again. He had learned his lesson. Henceforth stick with beer. Although at this moment, it was cool clear water from the creek that he needed to clean out his stomach. Once the sickly taste had been eradicated from his mouth, he felt much better. Yet still his eyes kept shifting towards the gruesome effigy perched atop the blackened husk of the wagon. A chilling shiver of dread rippled down his spine. Had he really been the perpetrator of this awful scene?

He couldn't wait to get away. Ben's horse was still waiting patiently where he had left it. Yesterday's grim finale had changed his life forever. In the cold light of day and thoroughly sobered up, killing a man no longer produced that feeling of glory and exhilaration he had expected. In truth, it elicited the solemn and grave reflection that he was also now a killer. And having taken the law into his own hands, a marked man, a felon on the run with a price on his head.

To be sure, the screwed up galoot had gotten his just deserts with Ben achieving the revenge he craved. But did it make him feel better, any more satisfied? That would need some serious thinking on. For now he needed to quit the scene of his actions pronto. Sooner or later somebody was bound to stumble across the charred remains of Deacon Crabbe. The old farmer as well as the bartender at the Arrow Head saloon in Broken Bow would be able to finger him due to the questions he had asked. Then the cat would be among the pigeons. The only safe course of action was to quit the state altogether. But where to go?

Ben immediately came to the obvious conclusion. Go find his brother. And that meant heading west across the endlessly rolling flatlands of the Great Plains. The last communication from Solomon had come from Deadwood. That was clearly the place to start. Maybe he would even meet up with Wild Bill. Without further ado, he packed up his meagre possessions and mounted up. A shiver rippled through his lean frame as he passed the charred remnants of the previous day's hideous conflict.

Ben had no real idea how long the journey would take, nor whether he was even heading in the right direction as he spurred the horse to a gentle canter. All he could do was keep following the sun and trust that Lady Luck would favour him with good fortune. He deserved it following the harrowing events of recent times.

In the heat of the moment he gave thanks for the good sense to search the drummer's wagon, requisitioning anything useful before consigning the whole caboodle to the torch. The five hundred bucks commandeered from the dead man's billfold could be regarded as expenses accrued. Yet in truth it was only an excuse and made him a thief as well as a killer. It was a thoroughly unsettling position in which to find yourself. But there was no sense mooning over what destiny had hurled his way. He just had to make the best of things.

At least the weather was calm. Nebraska was prone to strong winds hammering across the plains. These often developed into full blown twisters racing at terrifying speeds and destroying everything in their wake. All a farmer could do under such circumstances was batten down and sit it out, praying his crops would survive the onslaught. Ben prayed that he would not be caught in such an assault.

Over the next three weeks he made steady progress, calling at various homesteads and small settlements established along the scattered river valleys. And at each one he received a natural hospitality from folks eking out a precarious living in a hostile environment. Not everybody was like that blamed critter he had hunted down. And the notion gave him a warm glow inside. Here was the conquest of the American wild frontier shown at its very best.

Nevertheless, it was with a deep sigh of relief that he spotted a hand-painted sign pointing straight ahead that read *Territory of South Dakota – Four Miles.* The town of Whiteclay straddled the border.

And it was here while enjoying a celebratory glass of beer that he was advised to head north because of trouble brewing with the Oglala Sioux. This would involve traversing a notorious wilderness referred to as the Badlands. The tribes were irked at all the miners invading their lands in search of gold. And they were prepared to wage war on anybody foolish enough to get in their way. So the Badlands it had to be.

According to one old trapper who introduced himself merely as Pancake, the Badlands were well-named. 'A more bleak piece of dirt I ain't never encountered,' the old-timer warned. 'But if'n you want to keep your hair, it's the only way to reach the Black Hills country. Though I can't rightly blame them redskins for acting up. There's a heap of prospectors flooding into Deadwood eager to seek their fortunes in the diggings. They've just upped and ignored the government treaty banning any invasion of the Sioux homeland.'

'That's where I'm heading to find my brother,' Ben said. 'Sol left our farm six months ago to seek his fortune. And I'm hoping to join him.'

The trapper's eyes misted over as the recollection of fortunes won and lost passed across his mind. 'I sure had the gold bug when I was your age. Done my share of prospecting back in the first California rush of '49. Boy, those were exciting times. I wouldn't have missed it for anything. It gets into your blood, just like gambling. You can't stop. I'm just glad I got out in time before gold fever drove me crazy. Trapping beaver up in the mountains saved my bacon.' He fixed a caustic eye onto his young companion. 'You keep that in mind, young fella. It's only the lucky few that ever strike it rich.'

Ben was only listening with one ear. He was just glad to have left Nebraska behind. 'So which way should I head from here?' he asked, downing the last of his beer. He wanted to be hitting the trail. Far from dampening his ardour, Pancake had wetted his appetite.

'Five miles north of here you'll hit the Porcupine River. Just follow the left bank and you can't go wrong. You'll know the Badlands when you see them. Only a blind man could fail to spot that wasteland.' The trapper nodded his thanks when Ben set a full glass of beer in front of him. 'Much obliged,' he said, slurping a hefty dollop of the foaming brew before adding. 'And take plenty of water. Nothing can grow out there. Just keep following the setting sun and the chances are you'll make Buffalo Pass in four days.'

Pancake walked Ben out to his horse. 'Good luck to you, young fella. Reckon you're gonna need it. Take a break at Laughing Jackdaw's Trading Post before tackling the Badlands. Tell him I sent you and he won't overcharge for supplies.'

Old Pancake was spot on with his simple instructions. When the Porcupine merged with the White River, he crossed the shallows and continued onward. And that was when the colour of the terrain rapidly lost its verdant texture. Fading to a dull ochre, sand and stones quickly swallowed up the waving ocean of grass that characterised the Great Plains. He was on the edge of the notorious Badlands, and Pancake had also been right about the trading post.

Tucked up below a towering rampart of fractured rock were a cluster of wooden buildings. This had to be the Laughing Jackdaw. It comprised a stable, blacksmith's shop and a long cabin with bunkhouse tacked on the end. Ben nudged his horse over to join the other mounts tethered outside. He reckoned that a bit of rest and relaxation was needed before tackling the alleged harsh traverse of the Badlands.

Ben pushed open the door and entered a dim room, the walls of which were decorated with elk horns, buffalo robes, fox furs and other impedimenta testifying to the owner's previous occupation as a hunter. The man himself stood behind a bar comprised of long planks resting on upturned barrels. The grinning welcome for the newcomer certainly matched the establishment's colourful name.

'Come on in, stranger. Don't be shy,' the jovial proprietor espoused. 'There's always a cheery welcome for new customers to the Laughing Jackdaw. And the first drink is on the house.' The two other patrons turned to inspect the newcomer before continuing with their game of billiards.

'Got yourself a mighty fine place here,' Ben complimented the owner as he ambled across the hard-packed dirt floor admiring all the decorations. 'A glass of cold beer would sure go down a treat. Although I was always led to believe it was a Jackass that did all the laughing.'

'Not when your name is Dawson it don't.' The bluff owner chortled loudly as he pulled the drink.

'We also do a tasty beef chilli stew if'n you're hungry.'

'Might take you up on that,' Ben replied with a half-smile, thinking silently that the guy's horsy look and braying chortle was definitely more akin to a jackass.

Jackdaw set the foaming glass down on the bar top just as three men stamped into the room. They were led by a burly hardcase clad in a black leather vest and sporting a matching Stetson, the tall crown encased by a rattlesnake hat band. The other two presented an equally tough appearance. All three wore six-shooters tied down low. These jaspers were clearly not regular cowhands. And their surly, brash manner was intended to convey the message as to who was cock of the walk.

There was no hesitation as the leader stamped across to the bar, pushing Ben roughly aside. Without so much as a by your leave, the belligerent cuss then snatched up the glass, downing the contents in a single go before any objection could be raised. The beaming grin had slipped from Laughing Jack's face. He clearly knew these jaspers, judging by his diffident response. 'Ain't s-seen you in a wh-while, Buckshot,' Dawson stammered out.

'That's 'cos I ain't been round here, knuckle-head,' a gruff whiskey-soured voice growled out. 'Now set 'em up. Me and the boys have ridden a long way.' Buckshot Rodwell had earned an infamous reputation for robbing stagecoaches ruthlessly brandishing a Whitney shotgun, which he was not afraid to use. In consequence, he was wanted for

45

numerous killings across the northern territories. Rough mountainous terrain far from the reach of established law and order had thus far enabled him and his buddies to easily escape apprehension.

'Well don't just stand there, meathead.' The blunt order came from a stocky jasper boasting a white scar across his ugly kisser called Gash Blaine. Clear evidence enough of where his expertise lay was the huge Bowie knife strapped to his belt. 'Our craws are drier than a temperance hall. Ain't that the truth, Calico?' His grizzled pard slammed a fist down on the counter, nodding his agreement while revealing a set of tobacco-yellowed teeth through the grey of a thick straggly beard.

Initially wrong-footed by this sudden and rowdy incursion by the three cocksure braggarts, Ben stepped back unsure how to react. That was when the final remark from Wild Bill seared his incensed brain. *Don't let any man push you around, otherwise you'll always walk in the shadows.*

A cold-eyed look fastened on to the three intruders. Gritted teeth were set in a tight-lipped glower. His hand shot out, preventing Jackdaw from pouring the three shots of whiskey. 'I'm sure these gentlemen won't mind waiting until you've served me, barman.' The low yet poignant remark found the trio swinging to face this no account whippersnapper who had the barefaced cheek to confront the Rodwell Gang. 'After all, I was here first.' He signalled for Laughing Jack to pour the glass of beer.

Dawson sure wasn't laughing now. Sweat coated

his trembling brow, a quivering hand reaching for the beer pump. Ben somehow managed to maintain an outward display of calm intensity, although his guts were churning up inside. Levering himself off the bar, he prepared for the showdown he knew was inevitable. This would prove whether Ben Cade had absorbed the lessons taught by his mentor. A probing eye studied the reaction of the gang leader, who was somewhat nonplussed by this unexpected challenge to his assumed pre-eminence.

The billowing storm was not long in blowing up. The other patrons dropped to the floor, eager to avoid the discharge of flying lead as Rodwell's face warped into a snarling rage of hate. A growl akin to a simmering volcano rumbled in his throat. 'No darned runt of a kid orders Buckshot Rodwell around. You evidently don't know who you're dealing with here,' the owlhooter snarled as he also hunched down for the imminent face-off. His two buddies ranged themselves to one side, ready to back him up. 'I can handle this pipsqueak, boys,' he smirked.

Ben sucked in a deep breath. His whole body was tingling – in fear or exhilaration he could not have said. He had made his choice. Now he would have to live – or die – with it. 'It's your play. Ben Cade don't take shit from any rat-faced big mouth,' the young guy shot back, unsure if'n he had actually uttered such an incendiary provocation.

The insult struck home with a vengeance, producing another wrathful howl as Rodwell grabbed for his pistol. Ben judged the moment to perfection as his own hogleg appeared to leap into his right hand. Two shots rang out, both from one of Ben's revolvers, burying themselves in Rodwell's chest. The outlaw staggered back, a startled look cloaking the ashen face as he barged into Calico. The lumbering desperado tumbled over a spittoon.

Gash was quick to respond, drawing his own Remington. But Ben had anticipated the reaction and quickly swung the gun barrel, pumping another double tap that took the villain in the guts. Gash pitched over, groaning in agony, his whole system paralysed by the deadly hit. And just like Wild Bill had said, Ben took his time with the fifth bullet, effectively terminating the skunk's time on this earth. The gun now swung towards the quivering Calico, who lay splayed out on the floor. He was no hero and quickly raised his arms in surrender. Ben smiled. Three men down and one bullet left.

'Don't shoot, mister. I ain't gonna draw on you.' Calico's gaze fastened onto the Navy Colt, which looked like a cannon to his terrified peepers.

Ben took his time before answering. He needed his own nerves to settle. The second Navy was palmed to consolidate his winning hand. 'All I wanted was a quiet drink and you varmints had to go and spoil it.' He shook his head in mocking admonishment. 'You ought really to go join your pals in the fires of Hell.' A pause for reflection. 'But I'm no crazy gun-toter. So be on your way afore I change my mind. And you can tell folks out there what happens to jerks who rub

Ben Cade up the wrong way.'

Calico didn't need a second bidding. In no time, the thud of galloping hoofs announced his hurried departure. Just for the hell of it, Ben twirled the two pistols on his middle fingers before slotting them back into his belt. 'I'll take a bowl of that chilli when you're ready, Jackdaw,' he said to the trembling proprietor.

Ben was surprised that his voice sound so cool and unruffled. It was only later when he retired for the night that the consequences of his actions began to hit home. A tally of three deaths now lay at his door. Was this how life was going to pan out? In the cold reality of darkness, the uncertain life of a hard-bitten gunslinger did not seem so thrilling.

No time was wasted the next morning in continuing his journey across the Badlands. Due west from Laughing Jack's place, the rolling greenery of the plains was abruptly left behind. The bleak contrast was stark. From here on, turrets of rock interspersed with loose stony upgrades made for extremely arduous navigation. Plotting a course through this chaotic wasteland would tax all of Ben's skills. There were no tracks to follow and the chances of getting lost were high.

After two punishing days struggling against Mother Nature at her most extreme, he was wondering if'n it would have been easier to take his chances with the Indians. Too late for that now. All he could do was plough onward and pray he would emerge safe and sound on the far side. There was no let up.

It was the brutal contrast that sapped the energy of his mount. Up and down, up and down; steeply canting hillocks versus stark ravines twisted like impatient sidewinders to throw the traveller into merciless confusion.

Five days into this toughest of treks, Ben was leading his tired mount up yet another loose grade. Sweat was pouring off him in torrents. It was the luckiest of breaks the previous day that he had stumbled upon one of the rare springs to be found in the Badlands. Without that he would surely have perished in this godforsaken hell. Even so, the fearful thought was growing that he would never emerge alive. Twisting and turning amidst the labyrinthine jumble made it impossible to maintain a true course. Only the incessant blaze of the golden orb was able to point him in a general westerly direction.

Gasping for breath, he crested the hillock. Would it never end? And that was when he received a welcome surprise.

FIVE

BLACK HILLS
RECALL . . .

Below him, the ground levelled out for the next couple of miles, revealing a mist-shrouded line of uplands. The verdant sward was like an oasis, totally distinct from the bleak aridity of the last week.

These had to be the Black Hills – a rain-soaked region of pine forests. This was ideal terrain for fast-flowing creeks to wash out the gold depositing the valuable specks on gravel beds all ready for eager miners to gather up. That was the theory. In truth a great deal of back-breaking labour was required to flush out the precious reward in sufficient quantities to make it viable. Yet the lure of the yellow peril never failed to exert its mesmeric attraction.

Ben's jaded countenance lit up. Somewhere

51

within the confines of these hills was Deadwood. He soon picked up a wide trail well rutted by wagons and hundreds of excited gold seekers, each one hoping to make his fortune. All he had to do was follow where others had gone before.

And four days later a hint that he was nearing the town was verified by discarded debris scattered across this once untouched landscape. Soon after, a sprawling amalgam of rough-hewn wooden structures appeared, spreading along the bottom of Deadwood Gulch.

Ben's mouth opened wide. Never had he come across a burgeoning boom town in the making, and it was most definitely a shock to the system. Any image of rustic grandeur comprising a pine-clad utopia amidst soaring mountains had been stripped bare revealing barren slopes peppered with stumps. Numerous white canvas tents testified to newcomers awaiting the construction of more permanent premises. Colour offered by plants or painted buildings was absent. Everything was a drab grey. Here was a picture of gold mining in the raw.

Huge piles of discarded gravel tailings testified to the earliest gold discovery in the Black Hills. Huts erected amidst this chaotic confusion had now been displaced by a more permanent settlement. Once the easiest seams had been dug out, newcomers were forced up into the surrounding side valleys. Deadwood town had quickly become the hub where all manner of entertainment and equipment was offered, at a price of course. Gambling dens, cat houses and theatres vied for the miners' paydirt alongside general mercantile traders.

This particular newcomer nudged his horse along the main street, skirting the many ox-driven wagons delivering supplies. Of hunchbacked miners there was also a proliferation, many seeking solace from the never-ending toil in the numerous saloons. Every type of business was to be found here catering to the needs of these miners. Ben counted three Chinese laundries. At least the incomers appeared to have retained their pride to look presentable at the end of a long day.

Ben's primary aim was to find out where his brother had set up camp, and the best place to obtain that information was in a saloon. The first three proved disappointing. Nobody had heard of a Solomon Cade. It was only when he entered the Green Eye saloon that Ben received another shock. Thankfully on this occasion it was a pleasant one.

'I been wondering when you'd turn up here, young fella,' a familiar voice called out from across the crowded room. All eyes turned towards the door, loud conversation faded to a low murmur. That was always the way when Wild Bill Hickok made his presence felt. 'Come on over and join me.' Hickok then called across to Windy Wilson the bartender. 'A glass of cold beer for my friend. He sure looks like he could use one.'

Stunned by this sudden encounter with his boyhood hero, Ben took a moment to recover his wits before cutting a path through the smoke-laden atmosphere. Just like for Moses at the Red Sea, the milling throng parted to let him through to the back of the room where Hickok was overseeing a game of poker. The big man stood up and held out a welcoming hand. Envious eyes bulged at this familiarity from the notorious gunfighter. And to a jasper who bore all the hallmarks of a simple hayseed.

'Take my place, Slim,' Hickok said to the house gambler lounging against the bar. 'Me and my friend here have important business to discuss.' He then indicated for Ben to follow him into a back room. Once the door closed behind them, eager chatter broke out as to who this associate of Wild Bill's could possibly be. 'You sure don't let the grass grow under your feet, do you, Swiftnick*? A roadrunner don't have nothing on you,' the big man praised, offering a restrained smile. On witnessing the startled regard on the face of his companion, Bill filled him in. 'News like that always travels fast. And taking down two hard hats like Buckshot Rodwell and Gash Blaine has made you a star overnight.'

Ben was nonplussed. But he quickly hastened to assure his mentor that he had been literally pushed into defending himself. 'They forced my hand, Bill. So I took your advice and didn't take no sass. It surprised me how well I'd been taught. It must have

*The origin of the name *Swiftnick* comes from the true story of an English highwayman, the American version of which is explained in Derby John's Alibi, a Black Horse Western by Ethan Flagg (2014).

been Calico, the third member of the gang, who spread the word.'

'The scrawny runt passed through here three days ago bumming free drinks for his story.' Bill lit up a cigar, handing one to Ben. 'Your name is on everyone's lips now so you're gonna have to watch your back. Just like me. Take my word for it, having a reputation ain't all it's cracked up to be.'

Ben paused puffing on the cigar while musing on the dubious fame, the heavy burden that being a feared gun hand brought. He hadn't asked for it, nor could he discard it like an old coat. That said, he kind of liked having a nickname. And Swiftnick sounded good. Bill pushed a glass of whiskey across the table. 'Drink this. It'll help calm your nerves.'

Ben obeyed, even though the harsh taste was not to his liking. The over-indulgence of *Devil's Revenge* had seen to that. Nonetheless, the shot did indeed help to focus his mind. 'I came here looking for my brother, intending to make a fresh start,' he said somewhat morosely. 'But nobody seems to have heard of him.'

'Well that's where I can help you,' Bill enthused. 'I've been asking around and it seems that a Solomon Cade has headed further west over the border into Wyoming hoping to strike it rich in the more remote valleys. He let slip to a pal of mine over at the livery stable that a place called Blackwater Gulch is his destination. I ain't told nobody else.'

The information changed the worried expression to one of optimism. 'I'm obliged to you, Bill,' Ben thanked his benefactor profusely. 'Reckon I'll bed down in that flophouse I spotted on the outskirts of town then head off early tomorrow.'

'No need for you to be scratching your hide off in that flea pit.' Hickok tossed a key across the table. 'Use my room over at the National Hotel. I don't need it 'cos there's an all-night poker session on at the Brown Owl down the street.' The young man was dumbfounded by this tough hombre's open-handed generosity. 'No need to thank me,' Bill chuckled. 'Maybe you can repay the favour someday.' Then in a more serious vein added, 'Giving a helping hand to those in need is never a bad move. Remember that. It's one reason I'm still around and prospering.'

The two unlikely allies parted soon after; Bill heading back to his delayed poker hand, and Ben sauntering down the main street towards the National Hotel and a proper bed with springs and clean sheets. Dusk came early to the enclosed valley of Deadwood Gulch. Shadows crept furtively across the drab landscape as the sunlight faded to a purple haze.

Another day of fervent digging was coming to an end. Soon the miners would be crowding into the wide array of saloons eager to spend what paydirt they had accrued. Their less fortunate associates could only look on enviously hoping to cadge drinks when the hard liquor had tossed caution out the window.

Tallow lamps were lit in the variety of establishments lining the single street. But care was still needed to avoid injury tumbling over the numerous mounds of debris nobody had bothered to remove.

Ben reached the hotel unscathed wondering if his appropriation of the revered gunfighter's room would raise any questions. He need not have worried as the clerk was snoozing. He then crept up the stairs and entered room number six, to be met by a brand of luxury he had not encountered before. There was even a carpet on the floor. But it was the brass bedstead that drew his attention.

SIX

... AND REUNION

Ben was on his way well before first light so as not to encounter any problems from the hotel concierge. At the end of the town limits, the trail turned sharp left along a side valley where a few lone cabins clung to the hillside. Even at this early hour, lights could be seen as eager miners commenced another day of relentless toil to achieve their reward. It was clear that here was another mining settlement in the making. The rider continued heading in a general westerly direction away from the orange corona blossoming in the east.

On the third day he stopped at a horse ranch to find that he had already crossed the border into Wyoming. Enquiries from the owner informed him that Blackwater Gulch was only a half-day's ride up ahead. 'Watch for a distinctive landmark called Chimney Rock,' the rancher informed him. 'A narrow deer run heads left up through a steep bank of pine before levelling out. You'll find the gulch up ahead. What in tarnation you heading up there for?' the rancher enquired. 'Ain't nothing but trees and rock.'

Ben was ready with a suitable reply. 'I aim to do some hunting. The army is always happy to buy fresh game.' He had no intention of advertising the true nature of his quest. Too many over-chatty jaspers had inadvertently caused stampedes by blurting out their discoveries.

And so it came to pass that Ben Cade nervously found himself approaching a narrow gap that marked the entrance to Blackwater Gulch. Would his brother still be here? Halfway along the twisting creek he spotted a plume of smoke filtering out of the tree cover at the bottom of a shallow grade. Could this be it? There was clearly some human presence in this remote enclave. He pressed cautiously forward, searching eyes probing the dense cloak of pine.

Fifty yards short of the expected campsite he drew to a halt, calling out the customary greeting from a newcomer. 'Hello the camp!' Ben hollered. 'Rider coming in.' He then pushed forward, slowly at a walk so as not to alarm the present incumbent of Blackwater Gulch.

His first sighting was a white tent, beside which stood a tall man clad in rough working duds and holding a mug of steaming coffee. The pungent aroma of the strong brew reminded Ben that he had not tasted Arbuckles since leaving the Laughing Jackdaw. His stomach was rumbling like a rocky land-slide. Even beneath the thick matted beard and straggly black hair, Solomon Cade's craggy features were unmistakable. Ben's heart leapt. His brother was alive. 'That brew smells mighty good, Sol,' he espoused cheerily. 'Mind if'n I step down and join you?'

The camper's whole body stiffened. His hand dropped to the .36 Remington Rider he always wore. 'Stay right where you are, mister,' he barked out. 'And how in blue blazes do you know my name?'

Ben couldn't restrain a hearty guffaw. 'That's probably on account of us being related. Don't you recognize your own brother?'

Sol's mouth dropped open. 'Is that really you, Ben?' He didn't wait for an answer, hurrying on with more questions. 'How in thunder did you find me? And what you doing all the way out here?'

The elation at finding his brother safe and well was tempered by the grim nature of the visit. The smiled greeting fell from the younger man's face. 'It's a long story, brother,' he muttered, stepping down. 'I can explain everything better over a mug of that coffee.'

Sol ushered him into the camp, clearly overjoyed to see his younger kin. 'I can do better than that. We need to celebrate your arrival out here.' He went into the tent and brought out a bottle of the hard stuff. 'A generous shot of this will spice up that coffee.' The smile was instantly wiped from his face at the unexpected reaction to his magnanimous gesture. Snatching the bottle out of his hand, Ben hurled it against a boulder. Sol was totally flabbergasted by the sudden violence of his brother's abnormal behaviour. 'What in blue blazes is wrong with you, boy?' he railed impotently. 'Have you gone temperance or just plain crazy?'

The true explanation was not slow in emerging. 'I'm sorry about that, Sol. I just lost it for minute there,' Ben apologized, expressing his genuine contrition. 'It wasn't the whiskey, but the brand. I figured to have put the *Devil's Revenge* behind me when I left Gothenburg.'

'Reckon you need to open up, brother, and spill the whole darned episode.'

'Believe me, Sol, I intend to. And it ain't a pretty story.' A long draught of the strong coffee was needed before Ben felt able to launch into his disturbing tale. Though more than a tad bewildered by his brother's unexpected appearance and strange reaction, Sol didn't press for an immediate explanation, even though his impatience was hard to conceal. And once started Ben left nothing out, including his most recent fracas with Buckshot Rodwell and his gang.

Only then did Sol express shock at his younger brother's actions. 'If'n some other jasper had told me this I'd never have believed them,' he muttered, clearly amazed. 'Who'd have thought my kid brother who wouldn't say boo to a goose has gotten steel in his veins.' He shook his head. 'It sure is hard to credit. And meeting up with Wild Bill after all those stories we've both read about him. That sure makes me jealous.'

A coy smile graced Ben's sun-ripened face. 'They've even got to calling me Swiftnick.' Hands were lifted to show his apparent dismay. 'You gotta believe me, Sol,' Ben pleaded. 'That weren't my doing. Last thing I need is this kind of notoriety. But I couldn't let that skunk get away with killing Pa like that. When you never came to the funeral I didn't have no choice. And those varmints at Laughing Jack's needed cutting down to size as well.'

'I would have been there if'n I got your letter,' Sol butted in. 'This is the first I know about it. Poor old Pa. I know he liked a drop of the hard stuff, but he sure didn't deserve to go that way. You did the right thing in making that critter pay the full price.'

Following the bizarre revelations, the two Cade boys just sat there, gazing into the camp-fire while sipping their coffee. Each was contemplating the upshot of what the future now held for them. It was Ben who broke the silence. 'I meant what I said about helping you with the claim. Have you had any success?'

A gleam lit up Sol's grizzled face as he hauled out a leather pouch from his pocket. 'Take a look at this.' Ben's eyes widened as the sunlight glinted off the knobbly surface of a few small nuggets. 'And there's likely more of the same in the gravel beds I've been panning.' Ben gingerly fondled the objects that men were prepared to labour all the hours God sent to obtain. 'Problem is, for a man alone it's too much hard graft. But with two of us, we can build a long tom for sifting out far more gravel. I'll show you how it's done in the morning.'

Following a supper of fatback and beans washed down with more coffee, the two men settled down in the tent for the night.

Over the next few days, a long tom separator was constructed. Ben quickly learned the intricacies of sifting masses of ore-bearing gravel to extract the precious paydirt. The first few days were the hardest. It was tough work and at the end of each day both men slept like logs.

But they had been well prepared on the Nebraska homestead, where farm labour was likewise unremitting. Hand ploughing, seed planting, tending of crops and the final harvest required diligent effort to achieve any success. Wheat provided the highest cash return.

On first registering his land claim, a new farming settler would be advised to diversify into corn, hogs, flax, sheep and poultry, even bees for their honey. Few, however, took the advice. Seduced by a get-rich dream akin to those who headed for the gold fields, many sodbusters paid a heavy price when bad weather turned them into paupers. Jacob Cade was one of the wise ones.

His sudden and abhorrent passing was accordingly all the more difficult to accept, and Sol couldn't help berating himself for not being there to see him buried. A solemn assurance from Ben that it was not his fault helped some way to assuage the guilt threatening to overwhelm him.

Hard work was a sound panacea in that respect, but the take from the Blackwater site had thus far been small. Shifting tons of earth had hitherto failed to net the elusive reward. Sol was not deterred from abandoning the claim. The earlier finds were sufficient inducement that riches were there for the determined prospector. And so they continued. Steadily, with the two of them working in conjunction, a worthwhile quantity of dust was being amassed. And there was no denying the ripple of elation that finding even the tiniest flakes of gold brought to the young prospector.

It was at the beginning of the second week when Ben was in camp preparing the midday meal that two riders approached the campsite. Apart from his brother, this was the first sign of another human being that Ben had encountered since leaving the horse ranch close to the border with South Dakota. Curiosity rather than fear was outlined on his young face. Both men had clearly ridden far judging by the jaded nature of their mounts.

'Howdie there,' Ben greeted them. 'I've gotten some coffee on the boil if'n you'd care to step down. Looks like your cayuses would welcome a rest as well.'

Both men were in their middle thirties and had a hard-bitten look about them. The smiles wreathing stubble-coated faces did not quite reach their eyes. 'We're more interested in those fresh horses over yonder and reckoned an exchange is what's needed,' a tall rangy man with black hair and a scar on his cheek declared casually.

'I sure fancy that chestnut mare,' his buddy added, scratching his ear. He was a stocky jasper with sandy hair. 'We'll take the coffee and some of that grub as well.'

Ben's faced creased up. He immediately sensed trouble. There was no thank you or even the friendly greeting normally accepted among regular travellers. Ben was instantly on his guard. His body stiffened. But he was at a disadvantage. Unlike his brother, he had left his guns inside the tent. Nevertheless, he held his ground. 'The mounts ain't for trading.' The curt reply emerged as a throaty rasp. 'And I just withdrew the offer of vittles. Best be on your way.'

Scarface let out a mirthless laugh. 'Who in tarnation does this kid think he is? Figuring he can order us about,' he remarked to his sidekick. 'We ain't asking, kid. We're taking.' He dismounted, leaving his pard to keep watch.

Ben moved to bar his path to the horses. 'Not if'n Ben Cade has anything to do with it, you ain't,' he challenged. 'Some folks call me Swiftnick. And that ain't on account of any roadrunning talent. I tend to get awful mad when meatheads like you try pushing me around.' Ben squared his young shoulders. The run-in at the trading post had given him a brash degree of confidence when challenged by swaggering bully boys.

Sandy at least seemed impressed. He leaned across the neck of his horse. 'I heard about this jasper. Rumour has it he took out Buckshot Rodwell over at

Laughing Jackdaw's place.'

'It ain't no rumour,' Ben snapped. 'You can bet on that. And I don't cotton to skunks like you interrupting my hunting expedition.'

A mocking scoff came back from Scarface. 'You don't look that tough to me, kid. Especially seeing as you ain't packing no shooting irons.'

'He might not be, but I am.' The blunt challenge came from behind the pair of toughs where Sol had appeared. He was holding the Remington in one hand and a small Allen and Wheelock .28 pocket revolver in the other. 'Move a muscle, boys, and big mouth here gets a double load.'

Ben's stiff bearing relaxed as he silently thanked his brother for saving his bacon. His innards were still twisted in a tight ball but he was not about to let this pass without some retaliation. 'Pass me that Rider, Sol. Let's see if'n this meathead's bold words match his actions.' He slipped the large revolver into his belt. 'Your play . . . meathead.'

The colour had drained from Scarface's angst-ridden face. He held his arms wide. But he wasn't about to admit he was scared. 'You ain't gonna force my hand, Swiftnick,' he scoffed. 'I don't go in for killing boys.'

Ben gritted his teeth. But he was not prepared to let the threat from these varmints go unchallenged. He stepped forward and slammed a tight fist into the twisted kisser. The braggart staggered back, blood pumping from a split lip. His next growled command was for Sandy. 'Now get this dung heap out of here, pronto,' he said to the mounted rider, who hastened to bundle his sidekick onto his mount.

'I'll remember you,' Scarface espoused, rubbing his aching jaw.

'You do that,' Ben shot back as the riders spurred off. 'Next time I won't be so easy-going. You can bet on it.'

'Gee, Ben,' Sol gasped out when they were out of sight. 'I thought you were gonna drill the critter. What stopped you?'

'I didn't purposely go seeking to become a blamed gunfighter,' the younger Cade protested. 'It seems to have been thrust upon me. All I want is to live a quiet life until we've dug up enough gold to set us up for life so's we don't have to work our fingers to the bone no more. But when some critter comes along figuring to ride roughshod over me, I'm done letting it pass.'

'Well you sure chose the wrong guy to tussle with.'

Ben eyed his brother quizzically. 'Do you know him?'

'That's Blackie Crabbe. A real mean-eyed cuss in these parts. His pal goes under the handle of Bitter Creek Negus.'

Ben was instantly alert. 'Crabbe you say? Could be this jigger is related to that skunk of a whiskey drummer what killed Pa. His handle was Deacon Crabbe. It's an unusual name. I reckon this Blackie jasper must be his son.'

'Could be you're right,' Sol iterated. 'Blackie has a sideline peddling the hard stuff around here. I got my bottle in Sundance. It's the nearest town over the far side of the mountains yonder. And rumour has it that the Crabbes operate a distillery somewhere in the Bear Lodge range making the stuff. Nobody knows for sure. He keeps it secret from the authorities, but I heard tell it's somewhere up near a mountain called the Devil's Tower. That's where the name for the hooch comes from.'

'Looks like his pa has been travelling further afield with that darned sideline to bump off the poor suckers he blames for his misfortune at Pike's Peak,' Ben added, musing on the notion that Blackie had not yet learned his pa was dead, and that it was at his hands. Sooner or later that piece of news was bound to find its way into Wyoming. Then the cat would surely be among the pigeons.

Of all the places in America that darned hooch could have been made, it had to be here. Was that providence kicking him in the teeth, or just plain bad luck? Ben shook his head in frustration at the direction in which his life was moving.

Sol read his brother's thoughts. 'Lady Luck sure has a mean way of turning the tables when life becomes too straightforward,' he opined thoughtfully.

'You ain't kidding there, Sol,' Ben concurred, shrugging his shoulders. 'The Devil always finds a way of getting his revenge, one way or the other. We'll have to keep our eyes peeled from here on and hope this discovery of your'n pays off big time. Then we can skedaddle and find somewhere that don't harbour no demons.'

Over the next week the two brothers continued to work their claim, gradually building up a sizeable poke. 'Another few weeks of this and we'll be ready for cashing it in,' Ben enthused, eagerly studying his latest find. 'Ain't this the biggest chunk you ever did see?' The sun glinted off the rough edges, enhancing the brilliant golden hue. Mesmeric indeed. Was it any wonder that fellas pushed themselves to the limit to unearth such a dazzling find? 'Another few like this and we'll be set up for life.'

SEVEN

SUNDANCE SKIRMISH

Supplies were running low. Ben had delayed a visit to Sundance so as not to meet up with Blackie Crabbe. He had no wish to clash with the critter. Sol had offered to go but Ben didn't want his brother to think he was running scared.

'I've made out a list of what we'll need,' Ben said, consulting the scribbled note. 'All being well we can pack up and leave before they run out.' A dreamy look found him staring into the wild blue yonder. 'I've always had a hankering to visit California. Ain't never seen the big ocean I've heard so much about. And they reckon there's good farming country there. Growing oranges sure would suit me.' A wistful smile conjured up the kind of idyll all prospectors harbour yet so few bring to fruition. 'All we'd have to do is rake in the profits and become gentlemen of leisure. How do you fancy that, Sol?'

'Sounds good to me,' his brother replied enthusiastically. 'And to celebrate our good fortune, I want you to get in a couple of extras.' He then added them to the list.

Ben's face creased up in puzzlement. 'Peaches in cans? I never heard of that before. How do you get at them?'

'No idea. You'll have to ask the storekeeper.' Sol shrugged his shoulders. 'I read about them in the *Thunder Basin Courier*.'

'And cigarettes. What in tarnation are they?'

'Ready-rolled quirlies in a packet. Everybody's smoking them back East. If'n we're going to become men of means, we gotta move with the times,' Sol asserted. 'There'll be a whole load of other stuff to spend our dough on. Stuff to make life easier. I ain't getting any younger, boy. Don't I deserve some pampering?'

Ben was not fully convinced, but he understood his brother's reasoning. Both their folks had worked their fingers to the bone eking out a pittance and dying before their time. This gold strike would ensure their offspring could enjoy a longer and more bountiful life with the best that money could buy. 'From what you've said, I should be back day after tomorrow, with or without peaches or cigarettes.' Ben mounted up and spurred off, following Blackwater Creek to its source. From Skull Head Pass

71

it would then be all downhill to Sundance.

What he didn't know was that his every move was being followed by two hidden watchers. When Blackie Crabbe and his buddy had tried unsuccessfully to exchange horses with the alleged hunters, Negus had spotted signs that they were nothing of the kind. An abandoned gold sifting pan and rocker box, not to mention a shovel and pick axe, were dead giveaways. These guys were gold prospectors and clearly wanted to keep their business secret. The only reason for that had to be because they must have struck it rich.

It was good fortune that one of them was leaving camp on the day of their return to the remote gulch. 'That sucker Cade is leading a pack mule. Looks like he's going for supplies,' Negus said, making to rise.

'Not yet, pal,' Crabbe cautioned. 'Best we give the skunk time to quit the gulch before making our move.'

Negus settled down, watching carefully as the rider made his way along the winding course of the creek bottom. 'That sure was lucky me spotting their prospecting gear. Trying to make us think they were hunters,' he scoffed. 'They must have figured we were a right couple of patsies.' He slammed a bunched fist into his palm. 'Bad mistake. Now it's payback time.'

Fifteen minutes later, secure in the fact that Ben would not be returning anytime soon, the two bandits mounted up and made their way down towards the unsuspecting camp resident. Solomon

Cade was totally unaware of the threat that was fast approaching. Hungry peepers were avidly feasting on the results of the hard labour put in over the last couple of weeks.

All those months he had been slaving away alone barely making enough paydirt to keep him alive. Only when his brother had arrived were the two of them able to increase the output substantially. Then there was that fortuitous discovery of the ore pocket higher up the gulch, a stroke of good fortune that had netted nuggets of gold far bigger than any he had seen previously.

So caught up was Sol in emulating his brother's articulated aspirations that he failed to heed the imminent approach of danger. . . .

Ben slowed as he approached the town of Sundance. On this western side of the Black Hills, cattle ranching was a more prominent activity. Stores catering to the needs of the industry were much in evidence, not to mention the usual proliferation of saloons and dance halls. A couple of assay offices indicated that gold prospecting was still much in evidence. Unlike the blatant hells-a-poppin' saturnalia encountered in Deadwood, Sundance appeared to be more restrained, acting as a supply base for miners working in the surrounding hills as well as cattle men.

He drew the chestnut to a halt outside the first general store to catch his attention. The sign board read Zachariah Wilmott & Daughter – Purveyor of the finest produce. While tying up he couldn't help wondering if'n the daughter was young and if it was she who would serve him.

Ben had always been shy around girls, but that didn't mean he had forsaken the need to remedy that affliction. The store's dim interior was in marked contrast to the bright sunlight outside, yet he couldn't fail to notice the girl serving behind the counter, whose presence imbued a startling radiance to her mundane surroundings. Ben was instantly mesmerised.

A stray beam of sunlight caught her blonde hair. The effect was not unlike the first time Ben had handled that gold nugget on the edge of Blackwater Creek. This occasion was far more breathtaking. He was lost for words. The supply list clutched in his fist was all but forgotten.

'Can I help you, sir?' The question barely penetrated the young man's consciousness. All he could do was stand there like an awkward hayseed staring open-mouthed at this alluring fantasy. There was no doubting that Miss Wilmott was one very attractive young lady. Her whole being exuded a softly enchanting feminine appeal. Yet she was totally unaware of the startling impact her charisma had produced in the customer.

Again the request was repeated. 'I can see you have a list of goods.' A hand reached out. 'Perhaps if you would allow me, I could fulfil the order.' Vaguely, Ben handed it over, still enthralled by the silky smooth voice addressing him.

As the goods requested were placed steadily on the counter, Ben gradually came back down to earth. His somewhat naively innocent manner had attracted the attention of another customer who had been hovering close by. He was an older man, neat of appearance as opposed to the rough garb of a prospector. A slimy smirk creased the man's face, his thin moustache twitching with disdain as he watched the assumed greenhorn wrestling with the can of peaches.

'I reckon this fella must be new in from the boon-docks. What do you think, Effy?' the man posited in a barely concealed voice of derision.

The assistant sniffed imperiously. 'I'm sure the young man can answer for himself. Isn't that so, sir?'

Now fully aware of his surroundings and this jasper's mocking overtones, Ben's face broke into a bashful smile as he turned to face the speaker. 'Just come down from the hills, ma'am. Me and my pard are camped up there. We're hunting fresh game for the army.'

Ben then turned his attention to the supercilious dandy. He was not impressed. A jaundiced eye appraised the jasper's loud apparel, arriving at the conclusion that he was a gambler. The king of dia-monds stuck in a derby perched at a garish angle was a dead giveaway.

A close observer would have noticed that the smarmy dude had been less than happy with the stranger's obvious fixation towards the girl behind the counter. 'Allow me to assist,' he offered, taking hold of the tin. 'You'll need one of these to do the job properly.' A languid sigh accompanied the deft removal of the lid with a special can opener. 'Maybe I can also show you how to smoke a cigarette. So what's your name, country boy?'

Ben accepted the tin without comment. Extracting a jackknife from his boot sheath, he speared a chunk of the succulent fruit and chewed on it while holding the other man's lofty gaze with one of equal disdain. His reply was curt, direct. 'The name's Ben Cade, if'n it's any of your business. Some folks call me Swiftnick.'

The gambler was taken aback. The name of Swiftnick Cade had clearly struck a chord. Ben was instantly on his guard. News of his recent escapade at Laughing Jack's must have already crossed the border into Wyoming. But he did not allow his alarm to reveal itself. 'What's your'n then, cardsharp?' he snapped back.

'Chauncey Crabbe,' came back the hesitant reply. It was followed by a more wary postscript. 'I work the tables over at the Seven Stars saloon. Welcome to Sundance, Mister Cade.' Surprises were arriving thick and fast for the newcomer. Here was yet another blood kin of the critter he had hoped to have left back in Nebraska. Shrugging off the disquieting pronouncement, he added quickly, 'You related to Blackie Crabbe?'

The dealer's eyes widened. 'He's my brother. How come you know Blackie?' His cocksure demeanour had changed to one of wary suspicion.

Ben tipped the can to his mouth. drinking the delicious peach juice at his leisure before answering. 'I don't like him either.' There was no need to elaborate. Crabbe had gotten the message that somehow his brother had clashed with this enigmatic stranger. Any elaboration was cut short by Miss Wilmott announcing that the order was complete. 'How would you like to pay, Mister Cade?' she asked demurely. 'Cash or in gold dust. I have some scales over here and can offer you a good return.'

Mouth open, his reply was cut short by a flurry of gunshots outside in the street. All three hustled out onto the veranda to see what all the commotion was about. A short stout dude well-dressed in a more conventional manner emerged from the Seven Stars and hurried across the street. He was puffing hard and dabbing a handkerchief at his sweating red face, clearly unused to the exertion. 'What's happened over there, Mister Mayor?' Crabbe enquired. 'Ike Drago had too much to drink again?'

'This time he's gone too blamed far,' Mayor Scheffler gasped. 'The marshal went in there to calm him down and got shot up for his pains. He's dead. You're on speaking terms with that darned killer, Chauncey. How's about you wander over there and persuade the fool to give himself up.'

Crabbe quickly distanced himself from such a dangerous responsibility. 'No chance,' he declared. 'I value my health too much to tackle that crazy galoot.'

'How about you, mister?' the Mayor said to Ben. 'I'll swear you in to make it legal.'

77

Ben likewise declined the offer. 'I'm just here to pick up supplies. This ain't no business of mine.' He lifted the can of peaches ready to drink some more of the delicious nectar. It never reached his lips. A gun barked from across the street. The bullet was clearly aimed at the drinker and only missed the intended target by a whisker. The can exploded, despatching the contents every which way. But mostly over Ben.

Both the other men hit the deck in double-quick time.

Although totally bemused by this threat to life and limb, Ben still had the wherewithal to grab hold of Effy Wilmott and pull her down behind a barrel full of brooms. And just in the nick of time as another bullet smashed the store window where she had been standing seconds before.

'Sorry about that, ma'am,' he mumbled, suddenly aware that he was lying on top of the girl. The smell of her hair was intoxicating. Intermingled with the peach juice imbuing his own persona, it was a highly bizarre yet heady moment. All too quickly it was over as he quickly extricated himself, helping her up and through the open door to safety. 'There weren't no other way to prevent more blood being spilled,' was the contrite apology for his rough action.

Effy turned away to hide her confusion while brushing herself down. Her heart was beating a rapid tattoo like that of a Sioux war drum. And not just on account of the near-death experience. The closeness of this handsome stranger, his earthy smell, had affected her normally cool demeanour in a similar manner.

'You s-saved my l-life, sir,' she stammered out. 'And for that I cannot thank you enough.' The two young people stood there, feeling somewhat nervous and awkward. This was a new experience for them both. It was Effy who broke the uncomfortable silence that followed. Self-consciously, she held out a hand, which an equally red-faced Ben Cade accepted. 'I'm Estelle Wilmott, Effy to my friends. Perhaps you would agree to have supper with me this evening? An expression of thanks of course for your swift action,' she added quickly.

Ben took his hat off, shuffling nervously and trying to avoid focusing attention on his wet clothes. 'Be my pleasure, ma'am. Will your folks be joining us?' He hoped not. A solo meal with the lovely Effy would be worth this current aggravation.

The girl shook her head. 'Ma and Pa were taken by a cholera outbreak last year. I run the store by myself now.'

The private moment was bluntly interrupted by a jealous Chauncey Crabbe, who butted in with a sniggering piece of candour. 'Seems like Ike Drago has decided to make it your business, Cade.'

Still a mite shaky, but eager to consolidate his standing in the girl's eyes, Ben could only concur with the gambler's supposition as he surveyed the wretched state of his appearance and the peaches strewn across the floor. 'Guess you're right there. OK, Mayor,' he said. 'Give me the oath.'

'Good on you, mister,' the official voiced, relieved that somebody else was ready to stand up to the drunken killer. 'Raise your right hand ... By the authority vested in me I, Herman Scheffler Mayor of Sundance, do hereby appoint you as temporary marshal. And good luck to you.'

'Be careful, Ben,' Effy espoused, gripping his arm. Her touch sent a tingling ripple through his whole body. The young man's face lit up. 'That jasper is pure poison when he's in this state.'

'Don't worry none ... Effy.' Addressing the girl in this more familiar way put this budding relationship on a much closer footing. The peaches were forgotten. Arresting a wanted killer would substantially up his standing in her eyes. Settling his hat straight, Ben peered out of the door. Across the street all appeared quiet inside the Seven Stars. The proverbial calm before the storm, as Ben fully appreciated.

EIGHT

AN OFFER DECLINED . . .

The brutal truth remained, however, that a callous murderer was still in there and he needed flushing out. Ben suddenly cottoned to the hard fact that this was new territory for him. But he'd made his choice, sworn the oath. Backing out now would sour the respect he had accidently acquired, more importantly, his eminence in the eyes of Effy Wilmott. Girding himself up, Ben launched his lithe frame out of the door and dashed across the street.

He reached the edge of the opposite boardwalk unchallenged. Removing his hat, Ben slowly raised it. A bullet from the watching Ike Drago ricocheted off the wooden edge, snatching at the exposed head-wear. The killer was clearly alert enough to know his drink-induced killing spree would not pass without some response. Ben grunted as he stuck a finger through the singed hole.

This was no place to linger. He quickly scrambled crab-like along the lower edge of the boardwalk and up onto the stoop. Without pausing, he scooted across and through the door of the adjoining premises, which so happened to be that of a dressmaker. Two ladies were present, one clearly being fitted for a new dress. Both were cowering in a corner, terror written across their ashen faces. A suppressed scream emerged simultaneously from both customer and proprietor.

'Sorry to trouble you, ladies,' Ben hissed urgently. 'Is there a back way out of here?' A shaking finger pointed to the rear. 'Much obliged, ma'am,' was the brisk reply as Ben tipped his hat and hurried through to the back of the store. Emerging onto a back alley, he crept along to the next door giving access to the Seven Stars. A stack of empty beer barrels was enough to inform him this was the way inside.

Luckily, the door was unlocked. Silently he slid through and cat-footed across to the door giving access to the main body of the saloon. There he paused, an ear stuck against the wood panelling. A snarled oath from the killer on the far side was immediately followed by the crash of splintering glass. 'What you waiting for?' a heated voice bellowed out. 'Come and get me if'n any of you bastards have gotten the nerve.' The slurred voice had been scoured by too much bad whiskey. 'Ike Drago ain't scared of no darned critter in this shithole of a town.'

Gingerly, praying the hinges did not creak, Ben pushed open the door. Nothing happened. He breathed a sigh of relief, then peered around the edge. Apart from Drago, and the dead sheriff, the room was empty. All of Drago's attention was focused on the front street. He was swaying, a fresh bottle clutched in one hand, a revolver in the other.

Ben ducked down, slipping silently behind the long bar. There he paused to figure out how best to disarm this wild drunkard. He needed to get closer. Crouched on all fours, he moved to the end nearest the front window. Another pause to listen intently. The heavy, laboured breathing on the far side sounded very close. Extreme caution gripped his innards as he nervously peered around the edge.

Drago was still looking through the window, punching out abusive comments and hoping to egg the hidden townsfolk into winkling him out. Ben sensed that this was his chance, the only one he would get. He drew the Colt. It would be so easy to drill the varmint, but gunning down this poor sap was the last thing he wanted. No self-respecting guy wants to be labelled a cowardly backshooter. Just disable the fella and let somebody else handle the aftermath.

Fingers flexed, he stood up and tiptoed silently up behind the swaying drunkard. A light tap on the shoulder elicited a startled grunt as Drago lurched around. 'Who in hell's teeth are you?' he slurred, taken aback by this unexpected appearance.

'I'm the guardian angel sent here to prevent further bloodshed,' Ben casually whispered. Before the fella could respond, a solid right fist connected squarely with the jutting chin. Drago's head snapped back, bloodshot eyes glazing over. But he was one tough jasper and remained standing. Indeed the punch appeared to have sobered him up. A feral growl rumbled in the guy's throat, his gun rising to cut this tinsnip down to size.

Ben cursed, but this was no time for arguing. The Colt let rip. Drago emitted a pained howl, eyes rolling up into his head. Wobbly legs gave way as consciousness faded. Then he slumped to the floor. 'You durned fool,' Ben loudly berated the bleeding corpse. Another killing wasn't meant to be.

Ben rubbed his skinned knuckles before sucking in a deep lungful of air. Then, grabbing hold of the comatose body, he dragged it outside into the street. A collective intake of breath greeted the bizarre sight before the muttering crowd realized that the danger was over. Mayor Scheffler pushed his way through. 'Is he dead?' he said. It was a superfluous question. The quantity of blood draining into the sand meant that Ike Drago required the attention of an undertaker rather than a sawbones.

'The jasper wouldn't see sense,' Ben replied, attempting to justify himself. 'He didn't give me no choice. It was him or me.'

The mayor immediately called for some men to manhandle the killer down to the mortuary on the edge of town. Then he turned his attention back to the hero of the moment, who had been joined by a relieved Effy Wilmott. 'Don't you be worrying about that. Drago deserved all he got. You sure know how to take care of yourself, mister,' he congratulated the temporary lawman. The official then paused. 'But I don't even know your name.'

'Ben Cade,' was the blunt reply.

'And they call him Swiftnick,' interjected Chauncey Crabbe. 'He's the fella that took down Buckshot Rodwell.' A gasp arose from the gathered crowd. Everybody had heard about the notorious exploits of the Rodwell Gang. Some had even suffered at their expense. A universal murmur of approval greeted the surprising revelation, especially from the mayor.

But Crabbe had a further surprise in store for the unlikely hero of the hour. 'Not only that,' he announced raising a hand to quiet the muttering throng. 'I've just discovered that he surprised one of the Graystock brothers over in Spotted Horse. Shot Bart down stone dead with a single bullet in the forehead back of the Bighorn Corral.' Another gasp arose, all eyes focusing on the perpetrator of this bravura action as Crabbe waved the news sheet in the air. 'Those boys have been causing trouble all over Crook County.'

This time it was Ben who was dumbfounded. He spluttered, unable to voice his disquiet. Finally discovering his voice, he blurted out, 'That wasn't me. I've never heard of Bart Graystock nor have I been to a place called Spotted Horse.'

85

Crabbe was unconvinced. 'Here's the proof,' he insisted pushing the copy of the *Thunder Basin Courier* into Ben's hand. 'There,' he persisted jabbing a finger at the article. 'It's all down here in black and white. An eyewitness described the killer and named you.'

The mayor butted in, waving away the denial. 'No need to be ashamed. That critter and his kin have been suspected of claim jumping but nobody has been able to get any proof. You've done the territory a favour.'

Before Ben could further deny his involvement, the mayor declared, 'So how's about we make this a permanent job. It pays well and you'll get a percentage of all fines exacted from miscreants.' He aimed an expectant look at the young man of the moment. 'Now that Rocky Tancred has bitten the dust, you're just the kind of guy we need to keep Sundance in order. So what do you say? Is it a deal?'

Effy was also looking on, somewhat bewildered by all these revelations. She studied Ben with a troubled eye. Here was a man she had known barely an hour, yet was earnestly concerned for his well-being. He seemed so unlike the hard-bitten desperado depicted in the news sheet, not at all like those roughnecks normally associated with a gun-toting reputation.

But did she really want to be associated with a known gunslinger? Her smile was reserved, remote, not wishing to reveal the mixed feelings scooting around inside her pretty head. Ben was likewise hesitant but for a different reason. Suddenly that promised supper with Effy was forgotten as more pressing issues elbowed to the fore.

He had arrived in Sundance to collect supplies with the intention of making that last final push for the big pay-off in Blackwater Gulch before quitting and heading for California. Now he had been tarred with a killing of which he knew nothing and was completely innocent. The reason was obvious. Somebody patently wanted this Bart Graystock dead. And that person had carried out the murder and put the blame on his shoulders. Wild Bill had been right about a reputation tarring a man to such a degree that it became nigh on impossible to shuck.

Since meeting Effy Wilmott he would dearly love to have stuck around and prove he was not the gun-toting hardcase everyone thought. The fly in the ointment was the presence of the Crabbe brood. Sooner or later, word of their father's death at the hands of Swiftnick Ben Cade would filter down through the frontier grapevine.

And now there was this other killing. Would the remaining brothers avenge their dead kin by seeking him out? It was all a bit of a mess, a conundrum that needed thinking on – some time alone to work things out. The proposed move to California might now be a better bet than sticking around.

'Much as I appreciate the offer, reckon I'll have to pass on that, Mayor,' Ben espoused with regret. 'My brother and I have an agreement to supply fresh meat to the army and I wouldn't want to back out of that now.'

87

The mayor's beaming smile faltered. 'Sorry to hear that. Well, if'n you change your mind, let me know.' And with that he turned to address the crowd. 'OK folks, the excitement's over. Go about your business while I figure out who can replace poor old Rocky.'

Soon after, Ben and Effy were left alone in the middle of the street. 'Guess I'd better collect my supplies and head back to Blacktail Gulch,' he said somewhat lamely. 'My brother Sol will be wanting one of those new-fangled cigarettes.'

Effy was still in two minds. 'Will you be coming back to town soon?' was the diffident reply.

'I sure hope so,' he assured her, trying to hide the uncertainty clogging his judgment. 'But it might be some time. We're busy at the moment with all this hunting.' The awkward moment was curtailed as they returned to the store, Effy forcibly shrugging off her disappointment as Ben loaded up the pack mule.

All the way back to Blackwater Gulch, Ben's mind had been struggling to come to terms with the unsettling reputation he had inadvertently acquired. How would that affect his blossoming rapport with the delightful Effy Wilmott? He had sensed the girl's own indecision, the hesitancy in her behaviour towards him after hearing about the killing of Bart Graystock and the Rodwell crew. Added to that, niggling away in the background, was the noxious presence of the Crabbes.

With all this to occupy his thoughts, he soon found

himself in the enclosed gulch following the chattering creek up towards the campsite. The fact that
there was no fire nor any sign of his brother did not
register any concern to the younger Cade. Sol was
probably still working upstream. Only when he dismounted was the true horror of his brother's fate
revealed. Ben hurried across to the still form splayed
out behind the tent. A quick examination told him
that Sol had been dead for some time, and it was definitely no accident as the two bullet holes in his chest
proved.

Momentarily stunned by the grim discovery, Ben
vented his abject despair in a manic howl of anguish.
The chilling rattle echoed back from the towering
walls of the ravine. He slumped down onto his knees,
head bowed in deep sorrow. First his father, now his
brother. Could things get any worse? Only after he
had figured out the obvious reason for such a brutal
outcome did his anger know no bounds. All the gold
they had already amassed was gone, stolen by thieving murderers.

It was some time before Ben's distraught brain got
around to burying his brother. Slamming a pick axe
into the hard-baked earth gave vent to a deep frustration. Fate, providence, call it what you will,
appeared to be conspiring against the Cade family.
Sweat poured off him. But the tough physical graft
allowed the tightness possessing his whole being to
dissipate.

Reverently, he placed the cadaver into the hole,
muttering to himself about retribution as he filled it

in. Doom-laden destiny was repeating itself as he followed the same procedure, expressing the same banal platitudes over the makeshift grave. This occasion was immeasurably different in that he was the last member of the family to survive. Tears of regret, guilt and self-pity mingled with a fierce loathing for the skunks who had turned his life upside down in such a malicious way.

Standing there alone by the simple grave with head bowed, Ben promised himself that he would not suffer a similar brutal termination. The forlorn despondency was soon replaced by a burning spirit of determination, a resolve to exact a full reckoning from the perpetrators when he caught up with them.

And the only way to do that and also scotch the escalating notion that he was a ruthless desperado was to put the whole sorry business on a legal footing by accepting the mayor's offer of the marshal's job. Even though he had no experience of such a role, he was sure he could easily adapt and learn the ropes. Wild Bill had managed to successfully make the switch from gunfighter to lawman, why not Ben Cade?

NINE

. . . THEN ACCEPTED

All the way back to Sundance, Ben's whole being was focused on determining who had perpetrated the heinous crime. Even the delectable Effy Wilmott had been pushed into second place. He had his suspicions, but that was all they were. Who else besides Blackie Crabbe and his sidekick knew about the campsite in Blackwater Gulch? That said, the two ne'er-do-wells had given no hint of being aware of the true nature of the camp. Maybe their need for fresh horses was genuine. It could just as easily have been a passing drifter who had inadvertently stumbled across the gold claim.

Ben had no wish to take the law into his own hands, thus precipitating a further slide down the grease pole of lawlessness. Any attempt to achieve justice for the murder of his brother would need to be above board. Accordingly, his first call on arriving back in Sundance was to head straight for the mayor's office. Without knocking, he pushed open the door and barged inside. Scheffler was seated behind a large desk. His florid visage registered surprise at the unexpected interruption. 'I didn't expect to see you back here so soon,' he remarked.

Ben wasted no time on idle talk. 'Is that marshal's job still open?' he snapped.

A quizzical regard was the official's initial reaction. His eyebrows lifted. 'What's changed your mind? When I offered you the job before, you sure didn't snap my hand off. That army contract for fresh meat fallen through has it?'

'Something more important came up,' Ben hissed, gritting his teeth. 'Something that demands the full measure of the law.' Another puzzled frown creased the mayor's face as Ben added, 'Some rat killed my brother and stole all our goods.' No mention was made of the gold. 'And I've gotten a good idea who it was. So arresting the skunk will be my first job . . . if'n it's still open, of course.'

'Who is this guy?' the mayor asked, now all ears.

'You know a critter called Blackie Crabbe?'

The mayor nodded. A scowling grimace indicated he did not harbour a good opinion of the guy. 'He's the wayward brother of Chauncey Crabbe, who's the house dealer over at the Seven Stars. Blackie comes and goes. He always seems to have plenty of dough to throw around, and nobody seems to know where it comes from. Selling a few bottles of the hooch they make can't net him that much. But what I can't figure out is why would he have killed your brother just for a few haunches of venison?' Ben was still sticking with the concocted story about being a hunter.

He quickly explained the ugly run-in they had had with Crabbe and his buddy. 'When I refused to swap mounts he turned nasty and threatened to get even. But I never figured it would come down to murder. The guy must be one crazy jerk.'

Mayor Scheffler eyed the younger man closely before responding. 'I can sympathize with your loss, Ben. But you're gonna need more proof than mere supposition. This job is a lot more than just getting even. You need to be capable of enforcing all manner of statutes enacted by the territorial authorities. It's a responsible position. That's why it pays good money. Are you prepared for that?'

'I ain't done no law-enforcing before, but I sure am ready to do my duty,' Ben replied eagerly. 'Just give me the badge. You won't regret it.'

That was enough for Scheffler. He stood up. 'No need to repeat the oath of office. We already done that before. All I need to do now is hand you this.' He reached into a desk drawer and withdrew a shiny metal star. 'Pin this on . . . Marshal, and welcome to Sundance. Let's hope it will be a fruitful association for us all.' He then handed over a booklet. 'This is a brief list of all the duties expected from a territorial town marshal. Have a read through it and let me

93

know if'n you don't understand anything.'

Once the preliminaries had been conducted, the mayor informed his new employee that the law office included living quarters above. Before Ben left, he added with a brisk guffaw, 'Get yourself some new duds and charge it to the town council. We can't have our new law officer going about his duties looking and smelling like a hunter.' He smiled to show he meant the remark as a joke, even though his bulbous snout was twitching. 'And I reckon that a bath and hair trim will complete the transformation.'

It was a couple of hours later that Ben finally emerged from the barber's shop looking a changed man. Setting his new Stetson straight and adjusting the black necktie, the new marshal of Sundance made his way proudly across the street. His first port of call was the Wilmott general store. Ten minutes later he emerged grinning from ear to ear having convinced Effy that any reputation he had acquired was not of his making. A cleaned up Ben Cade clad in new duds had certainly helped to persuade her that any doubts she had harboured in that direction were ill-founded.

The tin star glinted in the sunlight as he sauntered down the street to visit his new office. Respectful greetings from numerous citizens were graciously accepted, but there were plenty of others who eyed him suspiciously. Sundance was a potent blend of miners and cowboys. Even at this time of day the town was a bustling hive of industry. For the first time in his life he occupied a position of authority. And it felt good as he proudly buffed up the revered badge of office pinned to his vest.

He passed the local blacksmith, who was hammering a new horseshoe into shape. A big jasper with muscles bulging from his sweating torso, Jake Ackermann, Hammerfall as he was generally known, paused to express his satisfaction that a new incumbent had been appointed. The positive endorsement, however, was tempered by a cogent warning.

'This town is going places, Marshal,' Ackermann stated. 'But make no mistake, you'll be kept mighty busy.' The cautionary advice was delivered seriously. 'The miners are usually OK when they ain't been overcharged. It's those mangy cowpokes you need to watch out for.' He scoffed out a derisive guffaw. 'Always looking for trouble. Seeing a new guy in the job they'll act tough, like overgrown kids trying it on with a new teacher. Make sure they know who's the boss and you won't go far wrong.'

'Obliged for the advice,' Ben replied, carrying on his way. 'I'll keep it in mind.' The young lawman was not worried. Since leaving his home patch in eastern Nebraska events had conspired to ensure the boy had quickly grown into a man. As regards the warning from the blacksmith, he didn't have long to wait.

Another block down he was about to pass the entrance to the Black Dog saloon when four skittish jaspers emerged. Judging by the raucous banter, they had clearly been drinking heavily. All were dressed in similar range garb – large bandannas slung around their necks, check flannel shirt, leather chaps, and high boots sporting jingle-bobbed spurs. Nobody could have mistaken them for anything other than cowboys passing through town before heading back to their home ranch.

One of them must have spotted the shiny new star and nudged his buddies. They all chuckled, eager for some fun at the new guy's expense. Ben moved to one side to pass them. His path was blocked by a bow-legged puncher whose scowling regard spoke volumes as to his intentions. Ignoring the obvious sign of impending trouble, Ben again tried to push past, only for another cowpoke to deliberately shoulder him aside. Caught off balance, Ben grabbed for a wooden upright to prevent a fall.

'That's mighty clumsy of you, Marshal,' the jostler, bald as a coot, decried grinning at his pals. 'Almost knocking me down like that. I reckon that deserves an apology, don't it boys?'

'You're sure right there, Bonehead,' a stocky roughneck known as Frisco sniggered. The others chuckled as Bonehead's hand reached out to assist the lawman into the street. Fully cognizant as to the quartet's object of mockery, Ben grabbed the arm and hauled the startled cowpoke forward, his bullet head connecting with the hard wood of the upright. The rabble-rouser tumbled into the dust groaning, and temporarily at least removed from the affray.

No time was wasted in checking the guy's condition, nor any petition for the others to see sense.

Verbal appeals to these rannigans were futile in a tussle induced by too much hard liquor. Swift and decisive action was needed to establish his credentials right from the start. All these critters understood was forceful and decisive retaliation. Accordingly, a solid right shot out, slamming Frisco back through the swing doors of the saloon. With the two main combatants out of the reckoning, the remaining pair of cowboys were too stunned to offer any form of back-up.

Ben didn't wait to find out. One of the Navy Colts leapt into his hand. The cross-drawn revolver swept up, cracking against a thick skull. The victim fell to the ground, leaving his pal open-mouthed, face white with fear as the gun barrel was stuck under his stubble-coated chin. Ben was in no mood for pussy-footing around. The cold gun metal roughly forced the guy's head back. In a low yet menacing voice, he hissed, 'You had enough, hotshot, or do I splatter your brains all over that back wall?' The hammer clicked back, an ominous sign that this was no idle threat.

The guy was quaking with fear. 'D-don't sh-shoot, Marshal,' he wailed. 'We didn't mean no harm. Just funnin' is all.'

'You see me laughing, big mouth?' was the acid rejoinder. 'Now pick this heap of trash up and all four of you get out of town pronto. I see you around before next week, I'll jail the lot of you for causing a public disturbance. Now git!'

No further encouragement was needed for the

survivor to brusquely manhandle his groaning pards onto their horses. Word would soon be passed around that you messed with this new lawdog at your peril. Ben felt the tension ease from his lithe frame. He had come through his first hurdle with flying colours. Realization as to what had just occurred dawned slowly. Ben gulped. Had he actually tackled four drunken cowpunchers and come out on top? There could be no disputing that in the last few weeks, mild-mannered Ben Cade, now known as Swiftnick, had certainly come of age.

He stuck the six-gun back in his belt. Only then did he take heed that a noteworthy silence had fallen across the main street of Sundance. The regular hustle and bustle had ceased as folks avidly watched how the incident would play out. Even the birds had abandoned their usual twittering discussions about the cost of bird seed. Attempting to effect a casual demeanour, Ben sauntered on down the street, looking neither to right nor left.

It was Hammerfall the blacksmith who broke the spell gripping the town. 'You done well, Marshal.' The praise conveyed to all and sundry in that the deep Texas drawl was warm and genuine. 'Old Rocky Tancred never did manage to tame those Box Elder braggarts. And you've gone done it on your first day in the job.' A murmur of agreement arose from the stunned throng as normal business was slowly resumed. 'Looks like you're the guy this town has been looking for.'

Ben nodded his thanks, entering his new office

and slumping down into a chair. More than a few deep breaths were required to steady his pounding heart. And just like the mayor had said, there was a heap more to keeping the peace than he had ever imagined. After the harrowing discovery of his dead brother, followed by his appointment as town marshal and the nail-biting incident with the Box Elder cowpokes, Ben suddenly felt exhausted. Swinging his boots up onto the scarred desktop, he was asleep in the blink of an eye.

Some hours later the snoozer was jerked awake by a timid knocking on the door. Rubbing the sleep from his gritty eyes, he mumbled a juicy oath before summoning the visitor to enter. Much to his surprise, a pair of young urchins shambled nervously inside. The elder of the duo couldn't have been more than ten years old. They just stood there tongue-tied, staring at the drowsy lawman. 'So what can I do for you guys?' the marshal asked, swinging his feet off the desk. 'Come to confess to a bank robbery?' A throaty chuckle followed the flippant remark. 'Or maybe it's just a stagecoach hold-up?'

'No, no, sir,' the senior visitor asserted, his eyes bulging in terror. 'It ain't nothing like that. Me and my brother Tommy here was wondering if'n you could use some help.' Both shuffled their feet nervously, the marshal looking from one to the other.

'We used to clean up for Marshal Tancred and make sure his duds were taken to Woo Ping's laundry,' the smaller of the pair, interceded not wishing to be left out. 'He weren't too fussy about his appearance. That's what Ma said.'

'He was an old drunk,' his brother Mike snorted. 'We both know that.' Straight away Mike knew he had talked out of turn. 'S-sorry for saying that, Marshal. It just slipped out,' he stammered anxiously, twisting his old battered hat.

Ben shrugged off the apology. 'Well I don't need any nurse maids to look after me,' he said firmly. 'But I could use a pair of sharp-eyed fellas to act as my lookouts.' He fastened a piercing gaze onto the two youngsters. 'It's a very important job. Much more so than cleaning up. You two up for that?'

Mike looked at his brother before answering for them both, a huge grin splitting his spotty countenance. 'We sure are, Marshal. You can count on us.'

'You sure can,' piped up young Tommy.

'So who am I employing here?'

'He's Tommy and I'm Mike. Our pa's the town blacksmith,' Mike said proudly. 'Any horse's tack or new shoes you need, let me know and I'll see you get a good price.'

'Astute businessmen as well as spies,' remarked an impressed Ben Cade. 'I've already met your pa. He's seems like a solid guy. So here's what I want you to do, starting right now. OK?' Both boys eagerly nodded their agreement. 'And if'n you do a good job, there'll be a bonus coming your way.' He then went on to explain the need for a regular lookout being kept on all newcomers entering Sundance. 'Reckon you can do that?' Eager nods from both employees. 'So get to it. And I'll be expecting regular reports.'

The Ackermann boys left the office with smug grins coating their young faces. Working as spies for the new marshal would certainly improve their status in the local pecking order. At the door, Mike paused, turning to address one final question to the lawman. 'Is it true what they're saying, Marshal? That you killed Buckshot Rodwell in a shoot-out?'

Ben was reluctant to accept the accolade but could not deny it either. 'It was either him or me, fellas. And Buckshot lost.' Open-mouthed with admiration, the two boys left the law office to begin their revered task.

Satisfied that he would not be caught wrong-footed by any hardcase wanting to cause trouble, Ben settled down once more to resume his disturbed slumber. He could not have guessed how long he had been under the influence of Morpheus before his eyes slowly opened. A much-needed stretch dispelled the stiffness from his muscles as he wandered over to peer out of the window. For a brief moment he couldn't figure out where he was. Then it all came flooding back. A sense of pride, excitement even, struggled to overshadow a deep sense of anger and distress. He shook off the conflicting sentiments. He had a job to do. But more importantly as far as he was concerned, a heinous wrong had to be righted.

Shadows of early evening were a stark indication of how long he had slept. What other sinister occurrences had taken place while he was out cold? Clearly nothing to warrant his intervention. A probing gaze panned along the opposite side of the street. An assay office, bookbinders, cattle feed store, the Red Dog saloon, butchers . . . That was when he paused, turning his attention back to the saloon. And there painted in red on a yellow background was the statement: *Now under the new management of Chauncey Crabbe.* It must have gone up while he slept.

Ben's whole body tensed. A sleep-induced lethargy was cast aside. How had a tinhorn gambler suddenly found the dough to buy a saloon? Gritted teeth suggested the obvious answer. This was enough proof that Blackie and his pal had carried out the robbery at Blackwater Gulch. They had then split the take with his brother. He was all set to march across there right now and challenge the skunk. Then one of Wild Bill's maxims nudged aside the rash move. *When pure anger to right a wrong rears its ugly head, take the time to work out the best course of action.*

So Ben sat down and did just that. Ten minutes later, he crossed the street, elbowed the batwings open and stepped inside the Red Dog. Ben looked around. Somebody had clearly been busy with a paint brush, the dominant colour naturally being a bright red. The place was full to bursting and nobody noticed the newcomer. They were all too busy taking advantage of the sign posted above the bar mirror: *All drinks half price until Saturday.*

But one person had certainly spotted the new law man. Chauncey Crabbe hustled across the room, barging patrons out of his way. 'Nice to see you, Marshal,' he declared breezily. 'Let me get you a drink.' He guided Ben over to the bar, where a couple of heavies elbowed out a place for the boss and his guest. 'Bottle of our finest whiskey over here, Rainbow,' he called across to the bartender. The hard-pressed beer-puller immediately abandoned his customer, much to the guy's loquacious displeasure. One of the toughs made it abundantly clear what would happen if the grumbling continued. The man instantly shut up and moved away.

'Not for me,' Ben said, trying to contain an angry retort when he eyeballed the bottle clutched in the barman's hand. He swallowed down a caustic retort. 'I only drink beer.'

'Then beer it is. See to it, Rainbow.'

Ben took a gulp of his drink while casting a critical eye over the room. 'Must have taken a heap of dough to set up a place like this,' he remarked in a deadpan tone. 'Bit much for a simple house gambler I'd have thought.'

'I've been saving all my winnings. Had a few extra good paydays recently,' was the direct reply, without so much as a flicker of guilt. 'Nothing wrong is there, Marshal? It's what all hard-working Americans want to do. Better themselves and start up their own business. Don't you agree?'

'You could be right, Mister Crabbe,' Ben said, struggling to hide a desire to floor the slimy dude. 'So long as the money is earned legitimately.' It was an inflammatory remark intended to rattle the gambler. And it worked.

Crabbe stiffened, rising to the bait. 'Are you accusing me of stealing the money to buy this place?

That's a serious charge to make.'

Ben raised his hands to placate the prickly dude. 'Just making an observation is all. No need to take offence.' The blank stare did not quite match the hint of amusement reflected in his sparkling gaze. Ben was enjoying himself at the gambler's expense. With barely a halt, he posed another query. 'What about Blackie? Is he in partnership with you?'

The saloon owner's blasé pretence slipped, the oily smile uncertain. 'Blackie looks after the production side of the business up at our distillery in the hills. He don't come down here much. Prefers to move around promoting our brand of whiskey. You might have heard of it – *Devil's Revenge*. A potent spirit and very popular.'

Ben almost allowed his own calm affectation to disintegrate at mention of the much-hated liquor. A few sips of beer helped to untangle his knotted guts. 'So when can I meet him?' Ben pressed.

The query put Crabbe on the defensive. 'Why you so interested in my brother? He hasn't done anything wrong, has he?'

'Can't rightly say at the moment,' Ben said, sipping his beer while holding the other man in a provocative gaze. 'As a new official, I want to meet everybody who comes to my attention' – he paused before adding – 'one way or another. You pass on the word.'

He finished the glass and set it down on the counter. Then, with a casual nod of thanks he turned and departed, leaving Chauncey Crabbe somewhat unsettled, nervy. He was not quite sure what the conversation had been about. Did the guy know something, or was he just fishing? Blackie had swore blind he had gotten the dough from an abandoned gold claim. The new saloon owner scratched his chin, a puzzled frown that did not pass unnoticed by his underlings.

'Some'n wrong, boss?' enquired a bearded tough going under the appropriate handle of Knuckles Muldoon. 'Is that tin star likely to cause trouble?'

Crabbe considered before answering. 'Nothing I can't handle. But we'll need to keep a watch on that guy. He ain't gonna be as accommodating as old Rocky Tancred.' He turned to the barman, nodding towards the bottle of best Scotch retained for his personal use. 'I need a slug of this to help me figure out our next move.'

TEN

THE DEVIL'S TOWER

By the middle of the following week Ben had settled into his new job. He was leafing through the latest wanted dodgers delivered on the weekly stage from Casper. One had Bart Graystock's ugly mush glowering from beneath the reward of five hundred dollars. He and his brothers were wanted for stagecoach robbery.

Ben chuckled to himself. The killer of the owlhoot must be cursing his bad luck not being able to claim that reward, having landed Swiftnick Ben Cade with the blame. When anybody mentioned the killing, Ben still maintained his innocence regarding the false allegation. His ruminations were interrupted by a knock on the door.

'Come in,' he called out, pushing the sheets into a drawer. His pleasure at seeing Effy Wilmott was tinged by a measure of puzzlement due to her being accompanied by a group of prim-faced chaperones. 'What can I do for you ladies?' he asked somewhat hesitantly.

It was Effy who had been chosen to be their spokeswoman due to her brief acquaintance with the marshal. 'My friends and I are members of the Sundance branch of the Women's Temperance League.' She paused to gather her thoughts together. Ben just sat there with his arms folded, a half-smile gracing his handsome features. Effy drew herself up, attempting to look more officious, but in the process merely succeeded in blushing under the new lawman's intense scrutiny.

A pinch-nosed older harridan sporting a ridiculous feathered hat nudged her in the back. 'Come along, dear. Tell the marshal what we want,' she snorted.

Effy coughed. 'Our view is that alcohol is turning this town into a latter-day Sodom and Gomorrah. Too many drunks have been harassing people going about their everyday activities.' Effy coughed to emphasise her contention. 'And you, Marshal, have personal experience of that to support our assertion. We want you to ban the sale of all alcoholic beverages in the saloons.' Her supporters vigorously nodded their agreement. 'Hear, hear!' they chorused.

Ben's eyes lifted skywards. Ban alcohol sales! He'd got more chance of bringing his poor dead brother back to life. He sucked in a deep breath before replying. 'Try enacting a law of that nature and I'd have a riot on my hands. There's no way menfolk around here would stand for it. And I don't blame them. I ain't no whiskey drinker, but I sure enjoy a glass of beer.' Indignant mutterings greeted this declaration. But it was the injured look of disappointment clouding Effy's sleek countenance that instantly made Ben feel sorry for her. 'What I can do is study the territorial guidelines and see if'n there's a ruling about alcohol sales that could be tightened. But I can't promise anything.'

He stood up, a signal that the meeting was at an end. 'I'll let Miss Wilmott know what I find out. Good day to you, ladies.' Then he ushered them outside, breathing a sigh of relief that it was over. Much as he did not wish to cause himself any unnecessary aggravation, Ben was still desirous of restoring his status in Effy's eyes. Consequently, he immediately dug out the guide to law enforcement given to him by Mayor Scheffler.

He quickly leafed through until he found the section dealing with alcohol. And that was when he discovered what might well be the answer to his dilemma. Section 5 paragraph 3 stated that any establishment selling whiskey from an independent distiller needed to register with the territorial legislature for a licence to prove it was of saleable quality. In other words, moonshine that had not been tested and approved was illegal.

Ben's eyes lit up. He had never heard of such a law before, and the chances were high that Chauncey Crabbe knew nothing about it either. This was a law of hope without any practical chance of application. Essentially there was no possibility of inspecting every functional moonshine set-up in Wyoming. The manpower required would be prohibitive.

Ben Cade was about to put his theory to the test. Abandoning the habit he had acquired of taking breakfast at the miners' chow house, Ben hustled straight across the street and knocked loudly on the closed door of the Red Dog. A further vigorous hammering was needed before a grumbling voice could be heard inside the saloon. 'Go away. We don't open for another hour.'

'You'll open to me,' Ben shouted, recognizing the gravelly tones of bartender Rainbow Fleck. 'This is Marshal Cade. Open this door pronto or I'll break it down.'

A sliding of bolts informed the visitor that his demand was being met. At the same time, Fleck had call for his boss to make his presence felt. Ben pushed his way inside just as Chauncey Crabbe appeared from a back room wiping his mouth. Ben smiled, pleased that he had interrupted the varmint's own breakfast. 'What's so important, Marshal, that you have to come here so early? Can't a fella enjoy his breakfast in peace?'

'Not if'n there's a territorial law being breached,' Ben snapped out, ardently praying that he was not about to make a fool of himself. 'Can I see your licence for selling registered liquor?' He held out a hand expectantly while earnestly watching for the scornful leer that would scuttle his plan.

Crabbe's ribbed forehead and stiff bearing were enough to indicate his plan had substance. 'What in thunderation you talking about?' he scoffed. 'I don't need a law to sell whiskey.'

'You do if'n it ain't officially registered.' Ben held out the guidelines. 'Section 5 paragraph 3. It's all there in black and white. I'm betting that your distillery making *Devil's Revenge* has never been checked and registered by the licensing authority. And it seems that I'm right.'

A blustering attempt to deny such a ruling existed was cut short by a sharp interjection from the lawman. 'Enough of this hogwash. I'm ordering you to remove all bottles of that damned poison from your shelves. Any attempt to sell it and you'll be under arrest. I'll be back later in the day to ensure my orders have been obeyed.'

'Why, you jumped up turnip,' Crabbe remonstrated, going for his gun. 'You'll never get away with this. There'll be a riot.'

Before the revolver was half out of its holster, a Navy Colt was pointing at his belly. 'I'd be within my rights to shoot you down here and now. But I'm giving you a chance to do the honourable thing and obey the law. You can sell beer and regulated whiskey, but not moonshine.' And with that he turned his back on the fuming saloon owner, accepting the risk of being shot in the back. Fortunately for him the brazen manner of his confrontation had caught the new saloon boss unprepared.

Ben left the Red Dog and went back to his office.

The much-anticipated breakfast would have to be postponed. Crabbe could have been arrested for threatening a law officer, but that didn't fit with his plans. Ben moved his chair across to the window so that he had a perfect view of the Red Dog's frontage.

Not more than fifteen minutes passed before Chauncey Crabbe emerged from the saloon and mounted up. Ben gritted his teeth. The critter was clearly heading up into rough country, having changed his usual flamboyant attire for well-worn range gear. It was also patently obvious where he was bound – the surreptitious location of the moonshine distillery. This was his chance to strike a telling blow against the odious cause of his father's premature demise. At the same time, what he had in mind would force Blackie Crabbe out into the open.

Two blows with one stone. No thought was given to the fact that he would be exceeding his jurisdiction, which officially ended at the town limits. Personal grievance had shouldered aside the oath of allegiance. Youthful ignorance of official consequences had effectively buried the warning from Mayor Scheffler regarding his duty of care to the town. Ben knew that he could have handed the problem over to the county sheriff, but that would take far too long, if'n it was tackled at all. Just like he had done to avenge his pa back in Nebraska, Ben intended going it alone.

The messenger was given five minutes to quit town before Ben followed at a discreet distance. This was new country to the vengeful shadow, as such he needed to keep the varmint in sight without exposing his presence and thus scuppering the plan to rid the territory of *Devil's Revenge* once and for all. So confident did Crabbe seem, he never once checked his back trail. But Ben was taking no excessive risks. He would only get one chance to stymie their heinous operation.

Herds of cattle were grazing contentedly as he passed through rolling grassland north-west of Sundance. The unsuspecting rider was clearly heading for the mountain country on the far side of the valley. After an hour the trail skirted the left shore of a lake where dense stands of pine dipped their roots in the lazy swell. Ben made sure he remained within the shadows of the tree cover until Crabbe veered off at the far side up a narrow gap into the rocky enclave beyond.

They continued to climb higher and Ben could feel a distinct chill in the air. He gave thanks that he had brought a fleece jacket, which he now donned. Twisting between surging turrets of rock, the careful pursuer was high enough to notice pockets of snow that the summer heat had failed to melt lodged in mountain crevices. Patches of swirling mist hovered around mountain peaks, imbuing them with a surreal air. It would have made for a stunningly beautiful sight had not the reason for the journey been an ever-present cause for concern for the resolute avenger's mind.

Ben congratulated himself on keeping a close watch on his quarry without the rat suspecting he was being tailed. Surely they had to be nearing the elusive hideout. And so it came to pass. Suddenly, on rounding the next bend in the trail, there it was. Directly ahead and unmistakeable – the Devil's Tower. Ben paused, gazing in awestruck wonder at the twin scimitars of rock arcing above the summit. The magnificent natural eminence was well named. Nobody who looked upon its demonic formation could remain in ignorance of their position.

And the overall setting was equally mesmeric. A small mountain lake lay basking in the sun, ringed by the ubiquitous guard of verdant pine tree sentinels. Somewhere lurking down there hidden amidst this unadulterated utopia was the odious distillery, a perfect location in which to produce moonshine whiskey.

Once again the odious vision of how Deacon Crabbe had abused his skill raised its ugly head. And now his equally scurrilous sons were continuing the family enterprise, totally ignorant of their father's demise. But for how long? Once again the certain assurance that news of that nature would surely penetrate this remote enclave precipitated a cold shiver down his spine.

Ben struggled to retain his vigilance. It would not do at this crucial stage to get cold feet and have his unwelcome presence placed in jeopardy.

He watched as Chauncey disappeared into the tree cover on the far side of the lake. Now that he had found the hidden site, Ben took his time. A slow yet focused approach found the pursuer on foot leading his horse along a forest trail beside a chattering creek. When he finally spotted the jumble of structures comprising the distillery, he realized the still itself was located in a separate building, removed from the log cabin that clearly housed the workers. Ben positioned himself on a ledge overlooking the encampment.

Two men were rolling a large barrel along to a place of storage. They were clad in leather aprons over dungarees. These must be the guys employed to make the finished product. Beer must also be made up here. That was of no interest to the watcher, the whiskey distillery was all that concerned him. A flinty gaze, cold and full of venom, settled on the wooden structure. Slowly his eyes shifted to the cabin, outside which five horses were picketed.

ELEVEN

HUMBLE PIE FOR BLACKIE

Chauncey Crabbe had joined his brother and Bitter Creek Negus. And with the two brew men, that made five in total working the operation. Ben smiled, imagining the heated discussion that was now taking place within.

The elder brother did not waste any time on banal pleasantries, instead launching into a tirade of recrimination. 'Do you know anything about some obscure territorial law that demands a licence for the sale of moonshine whiskey?' he hollered angrily at his startled kin. 'I've been ordered to stop selling our stuff by the new lawman until a licence is granted. And that could take months.'

A look of bafflement graced the leathery features of Blackie Crabbe. 'Is this some kinda sick joke?' he snapped back, rankled by his brother's animosity. The ugly snarl was answer enough. 'Of course, I don't know,' Blackie shot back. 'And what interfering bastard has given out such an order? That old soak Rocky Tancred would never have known about it.'

'The same one that shot down Ike Drago after he killed Tancred,' Chauncey sneered. 'And now he's taken Tancred's place as town marshal.' Blackie's startled look met that of his pal Negus as the string of events since the arrival of Ben Cade on the scene were quickly outlined. 'So now we've gotten this self-righteous hotshot running the place and threatening my plans to take over the town.' Chauncey stamped around the small cabin muttering and cursing as he tried to figure out some way to stem the rising tide running against him. 'He's even gotten Effy Wilmott eating out of his hand.'

Blackie couldn't suppress a wry smirk at this announcement, although he made sure his irate brother didn't see. 'So does this meddling snooper have a name?'

'Swiftnick Ben Cade,' Chauncey spat out. 'The kid just wandered into town asking about tinned peaches. Then he makes himself a hero by gunning down Drago.' He hawked out an angry lump of goo onto the dirt floor.

A distinctive recoil from both Blackie and his pal revealed to the older man that these two cheeseballs had come across Cade before. He had already suspected as much while bandying words with the guy in the Wilmott store. 'OK, out with it!' he rasped.

116

'When did you buzzards tangle with Cade?' A wagged finger brooked no chicanery. 'And don't try palming me off with some lame excuse. I want the truth.'

It was left to a morose Blackie Crabbe to explain their humiliating run-in at Blackwater Gulch and, much to his unease, their later return to exact revenge.

'So all that hogwash about buying an abandoned claim was a cover-up for you murdering Cade's brother for the gold?' Chauncey's blunt question did not need a response, the mortified looks said it all. 'You pair of bungling jackasses!' he railed. 'That's why he came back to Sundance and took on the marshal's job, so's he could make it legal when he guns you down.' The two buddies shuffled uncomfortably beneath Chauncey's castigation.

Much as he wanted to beat his inept brother to a pulp, Chauncey knew this was no time for futile recriminations. That could come later. After all, blood was always gonna be thicker than water. Now that the plain hard facts had been laid bare, the brains behind the operation knew more than ever how vital it was that Ben Cade had to be eliminated. He would have been even more determined had he known the fate of his wayward father.

Nevertheless, he couldn't help adding, 'And this sharp-shooting reputation he's been tagged with is no flash in the pan neither. The news sheet reported that he shot down Bart Graystock over in Spotted Horse. Avis and Reub are bound to be on the warpath when they hear about it.'

117

Seeing his chance to regain some much-needed standing, Negus interjected, 'That could be our ace in the hole, boss.'

'What you getting at?' Chauncey huffed, still feeling tetchy.

'If'n we get those boys to join up with us,' Negus put forward earnestly, 'we could run this bedbug out of Sundance and then elect our own lawman. One who'll be willing to toe the line.'

Blackie was not so keen on his pard's suggestion. His eyes registered a conspicuous anxiety, matched by a shuffling edginess. 'I don't know about that. Those fellas ain't exactly our bosom buddies.'

Negus gave the terse comment a disdainful grunt. 'What do you have against the Graystocks?' he snapped, somewhat peeved at his sidekick's strange reaction. 'Far as I can see, they ain't gotten no beef with us. My suggestion seems like a picture perfect answer to our problems.'

'That's 'cos you only joined us six months ago,' Chauncey interjected, aiming a caustic glower at his brother. 'This clumsy turnip' – he paused slinging an accusatory thumb at the culpable object of his derision – 'only went and soured his patch with them guys when he upset their plans to rob an army payroll shipment west of here in the Big Horn country.' He speared his younger kin with a jaundiced eye. 'You gonna tell Bitter Creek the ugly details, or am I?'

'It weren't my fault and you know it,' Blackie whined, struggling to retain his self-esteem. Not wishing his brother to pour any more humiliation on his head, Blackie launched into the sorry events of the failed robbery.

The five-man gang of road agents had been waiting at Busby Gap, which offered the ideal spot to waylay the wagon reputedly carrying upwards of twenty thousand dollars back pay for the troopers based at Fort Phil Kearny. He and a shifty-eyed weasel called Creepy Joe Dobbs were on one side of the Gap with the three Graystocks secreted opposite. When the wagon slowed to negotiate the narrow fissure, both factions were to have emerged guns blazing to cut down the accompanying escort of guards before they could retaliate.

It should have been the perfect heist, but nature in the form of an aggrieved rattlesnake had scuppered their plans. 'That damned snake spooked my horse,' Blackie espoused vehemently, trying to establish the truth of his conviction that he was not at fault. He grabbed up a bottle of *Devil's Revenge* to settle his nerves. 'It reared up at just the wrong moment and messed up the surprise attack. The escort were caught on the hop but were well trained and didn't panic. They shot straight and often. Creepy Joe went down and the Graystocks were forced back under cover.

'I managed to crawl behind some boulders and got off a few shots that kept those blue bellies occupied while Avis and his brothers were able to beat a humiliating retreat. We met up a couple of days later back in the hideout at Hole-in-the-Wall. Bart was all set to drill me there and then for ruining the heist.

Only the intervention of his brother saved my bacon when he successfully argued the snake attack was an unfortunate quirk of fate. And my covering fire had given them the chance to escape unharmed.

'Bart was not happy, but he had no choice. His brother's decision was final. It didn't make no difference though. That was the end of our association. And I ain't seen them since. Bart's final promise was to shoot me on sight the next time we met.'

'But he's dead,' Negus emphasized. 'And we know the whereabouts of his brother's killer. That will put Avis and Reub on our side.'

'Bitter Creek's right,' concurred Chauncey. 'And if'n we offer them a financial inducement from the profits of the distillery, I'm certain they'll agree.' Blackie was still rather sceptical, scared might be a more appropriate description, about meeting up with the Graystock boys again. But the line of reasoning from his two associates reluctantly brought him round. Chauncey topped up their glasses. 'A toast to a successful joint venture then,' he breezed.

'And the end of Swiftnick Ben Cade,' added a sneering Blackie Crabbe.

Three glasses clinked. Chauncey was confident that with the vengeful Graystocks on their side, Cade wouldn't stand a chance. 'Now that's been agreed, I reckon we ought to get moving,' he declared. 'The sooner we find those boys and offer them the proposition the better.' His next order was for Negus. 'You go and tell Enzo and Corncob to close down the still for the next week until we return. But don't let 'em in on the reason. We don't want this getting about.'

Before leaving the cabin, Negus posted a final question. 'When's Deacon due back from his latest expedition? He sure has been gone a spell.'

'That old scab is gonna get himself killed one of these days,' Blackie scoffed. 'Where's he gone this time, Chaunce?'

'Over Nebraska way. But he should have been back by now,' the elder Crabbe muttered cagily. 'You might be right about him overdoing it with that crazy notion he's harboured about Pike's Peak though.'

'Serve the crazy coot right if'n some jasper has sussed his game,' Blackie shot back. His father would clearly not be unduly missed.

'He's still our pa. So have some respect,' Chauncey reprimanded.

TWELVE

JOUSTING WITH THE DEVIL

Up on the rock ledge, Ben was still trying to figure out how to proceed further. Impatience was starting to make him edgy. That was the moment the three moonshiners emerged from the cabin. Negus went across and talked with the two helpers while the Crabbes mounted up awaiting his return. Then all three rode off at a crisp lick, clearly in a hurry. But instead of heading back down the outward trail, they headed off in the opposite direction.

A puzzled frown greeted the unexpected decision. Ben shrugged. The fact that they had quit the hide-away distillery was all that concerned him. His attention shifted to the pair of moonshiners. They had disappeared inside the distillery, and there they remained for the next half hour, leaving Ben impatiently cooling his heels unable to proceed with his plan. Just as he was about to move closer, the two men came out and also rode off, allowing the interloper a free hand to do his worst.

Wasting no further time, Ben dropped down to ground level and headed straight for the distillery. The door was closed but unlocked. After all, what chance was there of this remote hideaway ever being discovered except by accident? Carefully, he opened the door and stepped through into a different world. This was his first sight of a fully operational moonshine enterprise. The smell was the first thing that hit him, a distinctive aroma of fermenting sour mash and brewing beer.

Momentarily frozen to the spot, it took precious seconds for the sheer scale of the venture to strike home. No newcomer to the production of moonshine, Jacob Cade's meagre efforts paled into insignificance compared to this set-up. The place was filled with several large metal vats interlinked by an array of scrambled copper piping. Over on the far side were a range of different containers used in the large-scale brewing of beer. In the centre, sacks of rye grain were piled high. These guys were certainly well organized.

But not for much longer. Ben gritted his teeth. An all-consuming hatred threatened to overrule the need for caution. What truly made him see red, however, were the crated bottles already labelled with the detestable name of the finished product – *The Devil's Revenge*. And it was all due to the elder Crabbe's warped obsession, a mania that had twisted

123

his mind into hate-filled obsession about an alleged wrong committed at Pike's Peak in the distant past.

Ben had every intention of razing the entire caboodle to the ground. Fire was his chosen method of destruction.

The two workers appeared to have shut the enterprise down before leaving. It was a puzzling dilemma. What were the Crabbes up to? The question was put on hold while Ben searched around for the ingredients needed to terminate this operation permanently. Destruction of their illicit operation would force the skunks into a head-on confrontation – a showdown in which there could only be one winner. And Swiftnick Ben Cade intended to be that man.

He quickly uncovered a half dozen tubs of tallow oil used to fire up the boilers. More than enough to douse the whole structure. The mirthless leer written across the fire-raiser's grim features held no warmth. None would be needed once the flames did their work. He uncorked the first container and was about to start the process when he detected a flickering movement reflected in a window at the end of the building. Ben stopped abruptly, his whole body taut with unease. There it was again. This time he could make out a pair of hazy silhouettes standing in the doorway behind him.

For some reason those two distillery workers had returned and were sneaking up behind to catch him unawares. He had moments only in which to turn the tables. Effecting a casual disposition as if deciding where to start, he listened intently. A light shuffling of feet, barely audible, reached his straining ears. Judging the wary approach of the bushwhackers was crucial. At just the right moment, he swung around as the first man was about to lunge at him with a pitchfork. A quick sidestep threw the jasper off balance as he lumbered past.

The second man was already coming at him swinging a heavy iron bar. There was no time to dodge so he tossed the jar of tallow, forcing his attacker to duck. The fortunate lull gave Ben the chance to draw one of his pistols. Twice in rapid succession, orange flame lit up the dim interior of the barn, stopping the jigger in his tracks. But already the first man was back in the fray, jabbing the lethal prongs at this interloper.

Ben winced as a searing pain shot through his left side. Luckily it was only a flesh wound. He quickly backed off, covering the guy with his gun. 'Come any closer and you'll be joining your pal working for the Devil in his own playground.' The snappy warning was enough to stall the intended rush forward.

'Who in hell are you mister?' the irate worker demanded, weighing up his chances of regaining the upper hand. 'What's your game? You're trespassing on private property.' But seeing his friend lying in a spreading pool of his own blood had crushed any urge he might have retained to protect his employers' assets. The money they paid was good, but not enough to die for.

No opportunity was given for the man to regain

his nerve. 'Drop it, mister, or I fire,' Ben rasped, wagging the Colt to lend stress to the threat. The other Navy had now joined its partner. Ben's eyes glittered with malice as the hammer snapped back to full cock. He was watching for a reaction.

With two loaded guns pointing his way, the man's surly regard faded to a hesitant uncertainty. A further curt insistence saw the whiskey man abandoning the pitchfork. The submission added to Ben's growing confidence. 'I ought to take you in for operating an illegal still.' He tapped the badge pinned to his chest. 'But I ain't got time for hauling in small fry. I'm after the Crabbes, so it's your lucky day, fella, unlike your buddy here. So I'm prepared to be generous and let you go.' The stiff bearing of the still worker visibly slumped as all the fight went out of him. 'But if'n I see your miserable hide around here again, I'll shoot you on sight. Get my drift?'

'S-sure thing, Marshal. I know when to cut my losses,' he assured the lawman, arms still raised as he backed out the barn door. 'There's plenty other guys around here that could use a good whiskey distiller.'

Ben followed to ensure the brew man quit the hideout. 'Just make darned sure they have a territorial licence.' Once he had made certain the guy was not likely to return, he went back inside the barn with the intention of setting the saturated place ablaze. With match in hand, he was about to strike it when an obvious yet ignored corollary stayed his hand. A conflagration of this magnitude would produce a heap of smoke that would rise above the immediate tree line and be visible for miles around.

This abrupt realization was met with a rabid curse of frustration. 'Darn it!' he exclaimed aloud. Despatching the Devil's elixir to a flaming hell would have been the perfect act of retribution. So what now? The iron bar still clutched in the dead man's hand gave him the answer to his dilemma.

Grabbing it up, a systematic destruction of the whiskey-making equipment was soon under way. Crash! Bang! Wallop! Nary a single item was left untouched. Bottles, mash reservoirs, grain sacks, vats, barrels. Demolition of the much-hated, ready-labelled bottles depicting the odious *Devil's Revenge* accorded the wrecker a special form of macabre delight. 'Yahoooo!' he hollered out, venting his spleen. Even the beer-making enterprise was not left untouched.

By the time he was finished a half hour later, Ben was sweating buckets and breathing hard. The stink of fermenting corn and barley assailed his senses as he stood amidst the flooded barn. Expelled beer swirled around his boots. But there was a tight smile of vengeful satisfaction gracing the youthful features. When those varmints returned, they would be hopping mad. And that was just what he wanted. Destruction of the profitable enterprise would assuredly lure the killers of his brother out into the open.

And sure as day follows night, Swiftnick Ben Cade would be waiting to greet them – with a six-shooter in each hand. His aching body slumped down resting on his haunches. And that was what saved his life.

A bullet from behind winged across his back. The searing pain scorching the skin was ignored, an intrinsic need to survive the cowardly attack taking over. Ben twisted to one side grabbing for one of the Colts stuck in his belt and cursing his trusting nature. The spared distiller, Corndog, had obviously decided to avenge the death of his pal by sneaking back. It was only a helping hand from Lady Luck that had prevented the lily-livered skunk from achieving his devious intention.

Splayed out amidst the oozing mess, Ben triggered off two shots from the octagonal barrel. At the same instant, Corndog triggered off his own futile response. It missed, whining off a broken whiskey vat, and the backshooter then paid the price for his attempted bushwhacking.

Both bullets punched him back out of the barn, where he reeled drunkenly like he had imbibed too much of his own concoction. But he didn't go down. The dying brew man still had enough strength to raise the revolver. Ben wasted no time in idle speculation. Where had belief in his fellow man got him? Another two shots effectively terminated the craven attack.

The survivor's heart was pumping ten to the dozen. This was now the sixth notch he could have carved into his gun butt had that bizarre tradition invented by the dime novelists appealed to him. He shook his head, struggling to come to terms with the manner in which his life was heading.

Ben just sat there contemplating the chilling hand that fate had dealt him. It was right what Wild Bill had said – once you allow a gun to do your talking, it's like trying to bring a wild stallion under control. And it was all on account of those damned Crabbes. First the father and now the two blamed sons – Blackie and Chauncey. They were the ones who had caused him to take up the gun, and it was them who were going to pay the price.

A lurid curse hollered out like a raving banshee was despatched to the summit of the Tower. 'What's been done here is only the beginning of your troubles.' The manic promise bounced back off the enclosing rock walls, reminding Ben of the soggy mess into which his new duds had been transformed, precipitating another raging howl of anger.

Gradually the resentment blazing deep inside his very soul dispersed, the racing heartbeat settling to its habitual steady rhythm. Clarity and a rational gravity were once again able to assume control. Ben broadcast a silent prayer upstairs that chopping off the Devil's head would enable him to settle down, hopefully in the company of Effy Wilmott. That is if'n she would still have him.

But shucking the reputation of being a noted gunfighter was easier said than done. The simple life back in Nebraska suddenly did not seem so dull in comparison. Yet if he were honest with himself, Ben had to admit that the respect and deference accorded to guys like Wild Bill Hickok had its advantages. Folks looked at you in a different way, paid heed to your opinions. A sight more than when he had been a humble livery hand in Gothenburg.

Here he was now, the marshal of Sundance, Wyoming. It was a job that surely would not have come his way without that skill with a six-shooter. And it all stemmed from a chance meeting with Wild Bill Hickok.

Conversely, the notion that such a life could so easily be snuffed out with a single bullet was not lost on the young man. Would he have the nerve to face down three killers eager to wipe him out? The sight of his father's coffin being lowered into that lonely grave, and the odious reason behind the untimely demise, was enough to harden his resolve.

THIRTEEN

NO WAY BACK

Having emerged from the attempted ambush relatively unscathed, Ben's confidence had been visibly boosted. He now felt secure in his ability to handle any challenge those Crabby bastards made to remove the thorn in their flesh. Assuredly, they would be left in no doubt who had destroyed their lucrative business. And to make absolutely certain there was no mistake, he decided to take the bull by the horns.

A search of the place soon revealed want he wanted. Red paint and a brush – what more fitting colour to seal the defiant challenge. A deep breath accompanied the mute determination to throw caution to the four winds. For the briefest of moments hesitation stayed his hand. But what the heck, he had already burned his bridges. Might as well go the whole hog.

The message daubed on the barn door said it all.

A bleak sense of satisfaction suffused his whole being as he stood back to examine his handy work. And there it was in bright red. *Deacon won't be around anymore, boys. He's supping with the Devil.* The Crabbe patriarch was not coming home. Ben Cade had tossed his cap into the ring, a stark declaration of war had been given.

There could be no going back now. His eyes positively glittered at the thought of standing his ground and cutting these skunks down to size. Wild Bill had done his job well. No thought was given to the notion that he might emerge from the showdown a dead duck with his bullet-riddled corpse splayed across the main street of Sundance. Such was the blinkered, dogmatic attitude engendered by a youthful philosophy. Ben Cade would walk away victorious, his father and brother avenged.

Only when he mounted up did the reality of his situation begin to make itself felt. Stiff muscles vied with the more serious issue of the pain now asserting its presence across his back, where a searing bullet had scored a deep furrow, unseen but manifestly painful. He could feel the blood dribbling down his spine. And then there was the more obvious tear in his side from the pitchfork. Nothing could be done to staunch either injury. The only possible option was to get back to Sundance lickety split and seek medical help.

Much of the journey back to town was accomplished in a jagged haze of aches and pains. He sensed that his injuries were not life-threatening, but they were most certainly uncomfortable, throbbing and in need of tender care. And there was only one person he wanted to provide that benevolence and sympathy.

As he drew closer to his destination, Ben became ever more aware of his bedraggled, unsightly and smelly appearance. Not that he was overly concerned about what folks perceived, only how Effy Wilmott would react when he presented himself before her.

And he was not wrong in expecting the populace of Sundance to gape open-mouthed at the mounted scarecrow trundling slowly down the main street. Muttered comments and sneers were ignored. Ben's focused attention was reserved solely for the Wilmott general store. His two junior assistants were the ones who rushed to his aid when he almost fell off the chestnut outside the store. 'Gee, Marshal, what in seven bells have you been doing?' Tommy Ackermann blurted out as he and his brother grabbed a hold of the swaying lawman before he tumbled out of the saddle.

'Believe me, fellas,' he grunted. 'You're better off not knowing.'

On hearing the commotion on the stoop, Effy dashed outside. Shock at witnessing the alarming state of this salient if rather disquieting young man who had entered her life was immediately nullified by his urgent need of medical assistance. 'Get him inside quickly, boys,' she ordered bluntly, taking charge and leading the way into her private quarters.

There she saw him gently laid on the bed. Before commencing the delicate task, she gave them both a stick of candy apiece. 'I'll let you boys know the score when I've cleaned him up and tended his wounds.'

He could only smile, basking in the attention he was now receiving. The sight of this glorious vision fussing over him was worth all the discomfort he had been forced to bear on the journey back from the Devil's Tower. Nothing was said while Effy busied herself cleaning and bandaging the injuries. She also sprayed him liberally with sweet smelling unctions.

'A couple of days rest and you'll be good as new,' she declared finally, but her manner was stiff and somewhat reserved. A palpable atmosphere of hesitancy, uncertainty even, had fallen across what should have been an idyllic reunion. She turned her back to hide the doubt clouding her aquiline features.

Ben's initial euphoria had faded on discerning the chilly atmosphere. 'Something troubling you, Effy?' he asked somewhat feebly.

'I would have thought that was obvious,' came back the aloof reply. 'You come back here covered in dirt smelling like a pig and bleeding all over the place. Then you have the nerve to ask what's wrong. Don't you think I deserve an explanation?' All the while her voice had been rising to reflect her growing annoyance. 'I had thought we might have made a go of things, but you are proving to be just like all the other gun-happy drifters who have passed through Sundance.' She stamped her feet to emphasise the frustration threatening to burst forth. 'Well that's no use to me. Go get yourself killed. See if I care.'

But it was clear even to Ben Cade, a naive tender-foot where the female species was concerned, that she did care. The tears welling up in her eyes told him that some form of explanation was essential to calm the troubled waters.

'You're right that I didn't come to Sundance by accident,' he said, trying to repair the angst he had caused. 'I should have been honest and open with you from the start. But circumstances proved to be beyond my reckoning. If'n you'll hear me out, maybe you'll understand and give me another chance.' He waited on tenterhooks, praying this girl would offer the olive branch to redeem a soured reputation.

She was not about to make it easy for him, however. 'I'm going to finish off the work I was doing out front before you turned up. You'll have my answer when I return.' All Ben could do was lie back on the bed and live in the hope that his plea for understanding was not dismissed.

A full hour passed before Effy returned. 'Alright,' she snapped. 'Let's have it. And it better be good. I want the whole truth. Don't try any soft-soaping neither 'cos it won't wash.'

Ben heaved a sigh of relief before launching into his tale of woe. He did, however, brush over certain aspects of the grim revelation that certainly would have curdled his pitch, one such was the gruesome end for Deacon Crabbe. Impassioned stress was laid on the fact that he had not sought any of the notori-ety that was now his lot, especially where the killing of Bart Graystock was concerned.

'So there you have it,' he declared as the finale was related. 'These darned Crabbes have a lot to answer for. Someday soon, they'll be coming to confront me. It'll be me or them. And there ain't no way round that.' Although nothing outright was said regarding the manner in which the confrontation would be handled, the intimation was crystal clear. A gunfight where no quarter would be given.

'You could leave Sundance, go back to Nebraska and that farm your friend is looking after,' Effy suggested. 'I could sell up here and follow you. That way there would be no more killing. And we could be together.' Her earnest, emotive look beseeched this young man who had stolen her heart to see sense, to abandon this blinkered need for vengeance that could only lead to an early grave. 'There's three of them and only you, a man alone. What are the odds of coming out of that alive?' She turned away to hide the anguish bubbling inside.

Ben yearned to take her in his arms, but that way would only lead to his weakening and accepting her entreaty. He had to stand firm. How could a man live with himself knowing he had consciously allowed the Devil to have his way? Ben Cade had his pride. Without that, what was he? A husk, a mere shell, forever shouldering the heavy burden of betrayal and shame.

Squaring his shoulders, the marshal stood up and reached for the pair of Navy Colts lying on the bedside cabinet. He stuck them in his waistband, then set his hat straight. 'I'm obliged to you for looking out for me, Effy,' he said, his voice low yet insistent. 'But this is something that cannot be side-stepped.' He paused, attempting to swallow the lump in his throat. 'I can only hope that you'll still be waiting after. . . .' He left the inevitable conclusion hanging in the air.

Then turning on his heel he walked to the door. Effy's anguished reply struck him in the back. A searing epitaph riddled with equal measures of anger and distress as she finished off the corollary. '. . . waiting to bury you in the graveyard is all.' Then she disappeared into an adjoining room, once again leaving Ben alone with his thoughts.

He wasted no time in futile analysis of what he had decided. Instead, a purposeful step saw him heading across the street back to the office. Even now those critters could be heading for Sundance and he needed to prepare himself to receive them. Halfway across he was intercepted by Mayor Scheffler. 'What's this I been hearing about you having a run-in with somebody, Marshal?' He didn't wait for a reply. 'You were employed as a town lawman. Looking for trouble beyond the town limits is not in your juris-diction.'

'Just a little private business, Mayor,' Ben eschewed the query continuing on his way. 'Nothing for you to worry about.' He had no intention of elaborating. The truth would be out in the open soon enough.

'Remember what I said about settling personal vendettas, Cade,' Scheffler pressed home firmly. 'You have a duty to protect the town. Stick with that or find another job.'

A casual wave dismissed the official. Ben's attention was focused on more important issues. Already he could see the two Ackermann brothers waiting for him outside the law office. 'We been wondering what happened to you, Marshal,' Mike declared. 'Word on the street is that you've been in a fight.'

'Yeh Marshal!' young Tommy gushed. 'Did you gun him down?' He grabbed a wooden pistol from his belt and proceeded to blast away at some imaginary opponent. 'Bang! Bang! Gotcha mister,' he warbled.

'Cut the guff, Tommy. Marshal Cade wants men working for him, not kids.' Mike's rebuttal effectively cowed the younger boy. He handed the lawman a list of all the newcomers arriving in Sundance since their last meeting.

Ben rubbed the youngster's tousled head of unruly hair and smiled while perusing the list. Nobody of any significance caught his attention – only the usual influx of miners wanting to cash in their meagre pokes and a few cowboys asking after work on the ranches. He was also glad to hear that the Box Elder crew had not caused any more bother.

'You boys done well,' he praised them, handing over the agreed wages. 'But now I have a much more important job for you.' Both boys starred agape at this announcement. 'I want you to ride out to the north side of town and find yourselves a good place to keep watch on the trail heading down from the

Devil's Tower. Soon as you spot any riders coming in, get back here pronto. You fellas understand? I need plenty of advance warning to prepare a hot reception.'

'Is there gonna be a gunfight?' exclaimed a thoroughly animated Tommy Ackermann. 'Can we help out, Marshal? Me and Mike are both crack shots.'

'No way!' Ben avidly rebuffed the sincere offer. 'I don't want you boys anywhere near when the balloon goes up. And keep this under your hats. Nobody else must know. It's our secret, savvy?' Fervent nods assured the lawman of their discretion. 'OK. Now get going. I'll square it with your pa; tell him you're off camping out in the hills for a couple of days.'

FOURTEEN

CLOUDS GATHER. . . .

Once clear of the Devil's Tower, Blackie Crabbe informed his two pards that he reckoned the Graystock boys would still be based at their old hideout. 'That place ain't somewhere they would want to abandon,' Blackie explained eagerly. 'No posse has ever been able to find a way in. Hole-in-the-Wall is safer than our operation back yonder.' Had he known the truth of that belief, the lurid smirk gracing his warped profile would have been wiped clean. 'I'm one of the few jaspers who can breech that impregnable fortress,' he preened.

And so it proved. Another full day passed before the trio finally emerged from the brutal ramparts enclosing the hidden valley. 'Jeepers!' Negus exclaimed as the green spread opened up below the tortuous trail. 'I'd never have been able to find that gap in a million years.'

'Now you can cotton to why Avis will have only left here as a last resort,' Blackie replied gleefully. 'And we ain't heard any word that the law has got lucky.' He peered down at the herds of rustled cattle grazing on the rich pastureland awaiting sale to an unsuspecting buyer north of the border in Montana.

By midday they were approaching an isolated cabin secreted in a hollow. With Blackie in the lead, they slowed to a walk. 'I'll go in first,' he said, feeling a tad nervous now the moment of truth had arrived. 'It'll be best that he hears a familiar voice before you guys reveal yourselves.'

The others were more than happy for him to accept the risk of a bullet for his pains. They hung back as he nudged his horse out into the open. 'Hello the cabin,' he called out, his words husky with trepidation. 'Friendly rider coming in.'

Moments later, a rifle barrel immediately poked from one of the windows. At the same time, the door opened and a man stepped out also clutching a Henry repeater. 'Stay right where you are, mister,' a gruff voice ordered. 'State your business pronto or get blown out the saddle.'

Blackie's arms grabbed for the sky. 'It's me, Avis. Blackie Crabbe,' he croaked blurting out the reason for his unexpected appearance. 'I've gotten two pards with me. We have a proposition that you'll be interested in hearing about. I guarantee it.' He sat breathing hard, trying not to make his trembling

141

muscles evident to the hard-faced observer.

Avis Graystock just stood there frozen to the spot. Only his carbine displayed any sign of movement, much to Blackie's dismay. 'No need for any gunplay, Avis. Hear me out. I wouldn't have come here if'n it weren't important, would I?'

'It better be good, Blackie,' the elder Graystock growled. 'I ain't feeling too generous since my brother was gunned down.'

Seeing the relaxation of the outlaw's posture, Blackie nudged his horse closer. 'That's what me and my buddies are here for. We know where to find Bart's killer. We've gotten a beef against this varmint as well. So how's about we join forces?'

The startling revelation certainly had the expected effect, animating the suspicious gunman, who stepped out from beneath the veranda. 'This better not be some trick to collect the reward on my head.'

'It's right what my brother has told you, Mister Graystock,' Chauncey declared, making his presence known. 'We want your help in ridding our town of a troublesome parasite. You get revenge for your brother. And we rid Sundance of a troublemaking tin star.'

'OK, we'll hear you out,' Avis declared still keeping his gun at the ready. 'But keep those mitts high until I'm satisfied you're on the level.'

Once inside the cabin, the mood slowly relaxed over a glass of whiskey. The full measure of the proposal was outlined, with Chauncey sweetening the deal by offering Avis a cut of the profits once the moonshine operation was back in business with no more interference from Ben Cade. Mention of the gunslinger's name saw both Avis and Brad visibly stiffening. Neither man had read the latest edition of the *Thunder Basin Courier* in which the killing had been reported, but they had heard about his clash with the Rodwell Gang.

'So that skunk has built up his reputation even more by gunning down our brother,' Reub seethed, imbibing another slug of whiskey while he read the paper to his illiterate brother. 'He sure ain't gonna get away with that.' His eyes glittered with hatred. 'So what we waiting for?' He lurched to his feet, reaching for the rifle.

'Not so fast, little brother,' Avis cautioned with a raised hand. 'We ain't settled on our cut of the action yet.' He shifted his challenging gaze to the elder Crabbe. The older man now displayed his ruthless business sense. 'We want a half share in your business. Equal partners seeing as we're putting our lives on the line.'

'That ain't fair,' bleated Bitter Creek. 'It's us doing all the hard work.'

'Take it or leave it.' Avis rapped, knowing he held the whip hand. 'Now we know the name of the skunk who killed Bart, what's to stop us going after him on our ownsome. You need us to make sure this Swiftnick jigger don't rise from the dead.'

Unlike the Crabbes and their associate, the Graystock brothers were known to be competent gun handlers. Their back-up was essential for dealing

143

with a guy of Bed Cade's reputation. Reluctantly, they had no choice but to concur.

'Good decision, boys,' breezed a vibrant Avis Graystock. 'You won't regret it.'

Following a much-needed meal of fried potatoes and rustled beef steaks washed down with strong coffee, the five men left the small ranch house, heading back towards that narrow rift in the seeming impregnable barrier known as the Red Wall.

They reached the hideout below the Devil's Tower later that day, and that was when the brutal destruction of their whole enterprise was discovered. Anger and frustration left all five owlhooters fleetingly lost for words. It was eventually left to Chauncey to raise the roof with a lurid bout of cursing as to what would happen to the miscreant as he surveyed the wreckage and the red-painted message left by Ben. 'It has to be that damned blasted lawdog,' he railed impotently, hammering his fist on the barn wall.

'He must be the one who's done for Pa and his crazy obsession with Pike's Peak,' Blackie elaborated, more angry at the varmint's gall in trespassing on a family grievance than any concern for a dead parent. 'I'll skin the rat alive for this.'

'Looks like we ain't gonna be partners then,' Avis declared solemnly, more concerned about a lost opportunity for profit.

This was not what the Crabbe boys wanted to hear. 'I've got money stashed away,' Chauncey replied, simmering down. 'We can still pay you in hard cash.'

'You boys still want revenge on the varmint that

killed your brother,' Blackie cut in. 'And we now have a double reason for seeing him off. Plus the fact that we know Sundance better than you.'

Avis looked at his brother, who nodded his agreement. 'Guess you're right there, Blackie. It's too late in the day for carrying on now. Best we make ourselves comfortable in your cabin and set off at first light.'

FIFTEEN

. . . AS THE STORM
BREAKS

Next day Tommy was the first to spot the telltale sign of approaching riders along the trail. A plume of yellow dust rose above the line of confers some three miles distant like a smoke signal from an Indian fire. His small arm pointed. 'Somebody's a-coming,' he hollered out.

'We'll wait to see how many there are,' his brother Mike counselled. 'The marshal will want to know what he's up against.' At around the two-mile mark, the outlines of five riders could be seen plain as day. 'Alright, let's hit the trail,' Mike declared, slithering down the back slope of the ledge where they had established their lookout post.

No time was wasted in getting back to town. They hammered down the main street, weaving a danger-ous path between startled onlookers. Confused eyes followed the galloping duo with Tommy's strident voice urging them out the way. 'We gotta get to the marshal's office,' he bellowed in a shrill yelp. No thought was given to the planned secrecy of their task. Leaping off their horses, the two boys slammed into the office where Ben was busy cleaning his guns. 'They're here, Marshal,' Tommy blurted out. 'About two miles back up the trail.'

'How many are there?' Ben asked, expecting the answer to be three.

'We counted five,' butted in Mike. 'Do you need our help, Marshal?' he enquired hopefully, handling his Springfield rifle.

For a moment Ben was lost for words. *Five!* All he had been expecting were the two Crabbes and their sidekick, Bitter Creek Negus. Could these guys have nothing to do with the threat he was expecting?

'Can you describe them?' he snapped, ignoring the request.

'All I know for sure is that one of them was Blackie Crabbe,' Mike replied quickly. 'I'd know his ugly mug anywhere.'

So it was the Crabbes, and they'd managed to acquire back-up. Five against one were poor odds, but what option did he have but to face them? Running away with his tail between his legs was out of the question. For a lad raised on the harsh frontier of America's expanding western territories, such a course of action was unthinkable. He would rather go down fighting than slink away like a whipped cur to be forever shunned by all, known for the yellow streak down his back.

The anxious frown was replaced by a grim look of determination. 'You boys get back to your pa's black-smith shop and stay under cover. And tell everyone else to get off the street. There'll likely be a heap of bullets flying around before too long.' The goggle-eyed duo just stood there rigid, anchored to the spot. 'Go! Git now!' Ben rapped out. 'This ain't no place for hanging around.' Quickly he chivvied them out of the door.

Within minutes the busy street had emptied. Ben sucked in a deep breath. The pair of Navy Colts were checked. Then he selected a fully loaded Volcanic Arms .38 repeater. After jacking a round up the spout, he stepped out onto the street.

He was confronted by a ghost town. Only a lone dog chasing a cat disturbed the uncanny silence that had fallen over Sundance, the whole town appeared to be holding its breath. Yet Ben knew that a multi-tude of curious eyes were tagging his every move. Gunfights were best watched from the safety of cover.

The tight set of his leathery features registered the brutal fact that marshalling was a lonely job. When the chips were down, the man who chose to wear the tin star could only rely on himself. Lose and he would end up as just another forgotten graveyard marker, win through and he would be a feted hero, everybody's friend. Such was the way of the west. Which side of the tossed coin would fall to Ben Cade was now in the lap of the gods.

Slowly and with deliberation he moved to the

centre of the empty thoroughfare in a position where he could observe the far end of town where the gang would arrive. But an initial brash decision to challenge his five adversaries out in the open was quickly abandoned. Even Ben Cade knew that was a sure-fire way to a quick end.

Inside his rib cage, a tremulous heart was beating out a rapid tattoo, becoming ever more insistent as the minutes ticked by. He swallowed, struggling to keep a level head. It would be so easy to slink away with Effy, but sheer pride and the thought of his murdered kinfolk anchored him to the spot.

Then they were there, walking their horses in line abreast down the far end of the street. But there were only three. The immediate thought flashed through his simmering brain that two of the skunks had detoured to catch him unawares. Nervous eyes flicked to right and left trying to spot any suspicious movement. This was no place to loiter. Ducking low, he dashed across to the edge of the barber's shop.

And just in the nick of time. A screaming bullet whistled past his ear, smashing a window. Ben swung his rifle towards the puff of smoke on the far side of the street between the tinsmith's shop and the milliner's. He snapped off two rounds, driving the bushwhacker back down the alleyway. A quick look to the end of the street revealed no sign of the three decoys. Like spirits in the night they had disappeared.

A deadly game of cat and mouse was now afoot. Remain where he was and they would easily close him down. He needed to get away around the back of the main street and hope to catch them wrong-footed. It was a tall order but, as Wild Bill had stressed, attack was the best form of defence. If only the guy was here now.

He was given no chance for any further deliberation when a movement on the far side of a corral caught his attention. A man was creeping catlike along the edge of the fence over on his left. Before Ben could get off a shot, he dodged behind the stable. Ben ran parallel on the opposite side of the building with the intention of cutting him off when he emerged at the other end.

Both men sidled around opposite corners of the stable at the same time. Ben quickly eyeballed his opponent. Bitter Creek Negus immediately triggered off a couple of shots, but he had panicked and they went wide. Holding his nerve, Ben aimed for the gut. His first shot missed but a second struck home. Negus cried out, falling to his knees. He tried lifting the Remington clutched in his hand, but it was too late. The gut shot had paralyzed his system, giving Ben the chance to finish the contest. It was a coolly delivered shot. Negus keeled over and lay still.

Ben did not feel any elation, only an emptiness that yet another human being had fallen to his gun hand. There were still four killers out there all wanting to fill his hide with lead. And they would now be converging, having heard the short-lived gun battle. An urgent need to vacate the scene of conflict found him scuttling away hoping to have a similar piece of good fortune at his next encounter.

And none too soon. He was forced to zig-zag across the open sward as bullets kicked up sand between his flying boot heels. One plucked at his sleeve moments before he tumbled headlong behind a stack of barrels.

Wheezing heavily, he paused to draw breath, then cursed. Somehow the Volcanic rifle had been ditched in the dash for safety. With only hand guns for protection, he would be safer on the main street where there was less chance of being caught in a tricky situation. Cautiously, he edged along the boardwalk past the dressmaker's window through which anxious female faces could be discerned. And there he was suddenly confronted by an adversary he had never seen before.

Both men locked eyes. It was the other jigger who made the first move as he stepped out from an alley-way into full view. An accusatory finger pointed at Ben. 'You're the yellow rat who gunned down my brother,' Reub Graystock snarled angrily, settling himself into the classic gunfighter's stance. Legs akimbo and slightly bent, gun arm raised ready for the draw, he called out, 'Now I'm gonna settle the score. But I'm giving you an even shake, unlike what you did for Bart.'

Ben froze dumbfounded. So those two sidekicks were the Graystock brothers. Even though he knew a showdown was inevitable, he still needed to press home his innocence and quickly found his voice to utter a vehement protestation. 'That wasn't me, fella.

I've never met your brother. Someone else killed him and saddled me with the blame.'

'You're a lying scumbag. The whole thing was reported in the *Courier*. So don't even try denying it.'

'Your brother must have made an enemy of some other jasper. It sure weren't me.' Ben did not realize that Reub Graystock had made his presence known as a scheming ploy to give his elder kin the chance to drill the skunk from behind.

Avis had stepped out from where he had been watching proceedings from the shelter of the Red Dog saloon doorway. An evil smile, coldly malicious and totally devoid of any gallantry, distorted the elder Graystock's ugly scowling mush. His gun hand rose to deliver the *coup de grace*. The outlaw harboured not the slightest compunction about delivering a cowardly back shot.

As his finger tightened on the trigger he was punched back through the batwings. Startled onlookers stepped briskly out of his way, starring open-mouthed at the twin holes in his chest, both pumping blood. They were killing shots dispensed by a single Navy Colt held in the hand of a tall buckskin-clad gunslinger with long golden hair and that trademark moustache and beard.

'I don't cotton to backshooters,' Wild Bill intoned, his eyes scanning the street for other wayward aggressors. 'Never have, never will. Think you can take this turkey, Ben?' His gaze fell upon the stunned figure of Reub Graystock. 'I'll cover you from over here to make sure nobody interferes.'

Ben was equally stunned at the unexpected but no less welcome appearance of his mentor. 'Boy, I sure am glad to see you, Bill,' he declared. 'What's brought you to Sundance?'

'Heard tell you had been lumbered with a false accusation and might need some help when these boys came a-hunting. And it looks like there's still a bit of clearing up to be done. So, are you able to handle this jasper?'

Ben gritted his teeth, turning back to face the anxious younger Graystock. 'Your play, mister. But I don't favour your odds of walking away. Being carried down to the undertaker is a more likely outcome.'

Just like his elder brother, Reub Graystock did not take unnecessary risks, always playing from a stacked deck. He threw down his gun and backed off. 'I ain't gonna draw on you, Cade. I believe you when you say you didn't kill Bart. So I'm done here.' Hands in the air he turned and hurried off.

But there were others still in the fray who had no intention of permitting any kind of surrender by the lily-livered owlhoot. A gun blasted from a veranda above the Red Dog. 'Nobody quits on me,' hollered Chauncey Crabbe. Before either Cade or Hickok could reply he had disappeared back inside the saloon.

'Looks like we've still gotten some winkling out to do, Ben,' Hickok sniggered across to his associate. 'How many more are left?'

'Apart from Chauncey, his brother Blackie is skulking around here somewhere,' Ben replied. Then in a louder voice intended to carry, he called out, 'Why don't you show yourself, Blackie? Come out and face me like a man.' The reaction was a blast of gunfire from further down the street that chewed slivers of wood inches from Ben's head, forcing him to duck. 'Guess I'm gonna have to do some winkling as well,' he added, meeting Wild Bill's macabre grin with a more hesitant twist of the lip.

'You can easily deal with scum that ain't gotten the guts for a proper fight,' Bill replied. 'Go take him, boy. I'll manage Crabbe the Elder.'

SIXTEEN

FINAL THROW OF THE DICE

An eager nod saw Ben surreptitiously moving off. The notion entered his head that he was beginning to enjoy himself. Perhaps it was the jubilation of having Wild Bill Hickok come to his aid, or had he gotten a morbid taste for killing? That notion was somewhat disquieting. But this was no time for deliberating the veracity of such fatalistic machinations, there was still the thorny matter of finding and neutralizing Blackie Crabbe.

With more confidence than he had before the battle – little more than fifteen minutes since yet it seemed like half a lifetime – Ben commandeered an abandoned wagon with the team of four still in the traces. Slapping the leathers, he urged the team up to the gallop. His intention was to catch the younger

Crabbe out in the open behind the main block and take him by surprise.

He swung the wagon in a slurring wheel down the side street from where the gunfire had originated. And there he was, scurrying across the back lot making for the rear of the Red Dog to join his brother. Emitting an exuberant 'Yahoooooo!' Ben urged the hurtling wagon across the open sward, bearing down on the fleeing villain. Drawing level, he hauled back on the reins and threw himself at the startled outlaw.

Both men crashed to the ground in a welter of tangled arms and legs, but Blackie was first on his feet. He swung a bunched fist at Ben, catching him high on the head. It was a solid blow that stunned the young lawman, but he was still sufficiently cognizant to know he was in great danger and scrambled under the bed of the now static wagon before Blackie could draw his pistol.

Shaking his head to clear the threatened stupor, Ben drew his own weapon and circled around the end of the wagon keeping his head below the parapet. He was breathing hard, exhilaration blending with anxiety-laced tension. He paused listening. Blackie was on the far side, likewise circling around. Silently, Ben lifted himself into the bed of the empty wagon and crawled forward to where he figured his adversary was waiting. Girding up his loins, he stood up.

Blackie was sneaking around to where Ben had been crouched moments before and had his back to him. 'Drop the gun, Blackie,' he rasped. 'You're under arrest for the murder of my brother and for running an illegal whiskey distillery.'

Caught wrong-footed, Blackie knew his goose was cooked. But the wrecking of the distillery in all its grotesque detail was too vividly imprinted on his conscience. No thought could be given to any form of capitulation now; rage at this infuriating interloper was too deeply embedded. It burst forth in a bestial growl of hate as he swung around, his shooter rising.

Ben was ready. His own gun bucked three times in his fist. Blam! Blam! Blam! Barely any space separated the triple punctures in the victim's chest. White smoke twined from the barrel as he watched Blackie slowly sink to the ground. A last deathly twitch registered the futile end of a life lived on the wrong side of the tracks. The survivor quickly rushed back onto the main street, hurrying over to the Red Dog. No shots had been heard coming from inside the saloon, which signified that Wild Bill had still not yet caught up with his prey.

That was when Effy Wilmott emerged from the general store. On seeing that Ben was still very much alive, she gasped out in relief. 'Thank the Lord you have been spared,' she gushed, hurrying forward to embrace him. 'With all that shooting going on, I felt certain they would have killed you.'

'There's still time for that, lady,' a menacing growl was uttered by Chauncey Crabbe as he cut her off, grabbing her around the waist. A pistol was jammed into the side of Effy's head. The painful jab elicited a terrified scream from her lips at the sudden shock of being held hostage. 'Back off, Cade, or the girl gets it.'

Chauncey had abandoned the saloon knowing that Wild Bill Hickok was on his tail. Once he realized that the game was well and truly up, the need to alter his plans quickly became an urgent priority. And Effy Wilmott was the key to a safe escape. By holding her to ransom, he would have a bargaining chip. The heavy saddle-bag slung over his shoulder contained most of the money he had acquired from selling the gold stolen at Blackwater Gulch. Thankfully only a deposit had so far been paid over to the bank.

Only Chauncey was left now, and he intended to make good his escape over the border and disappear. Neither the celebrated ladies' man Hickok nor the intruder Cade would want any harm to come to the girl. He could easily abandon her once he felt safe from pursuit. 'Go bring my horse from outside the saloon,' he ordered the marshal, twisting a cry of pain from the girl to ensure obedience to his curt demand. 'Try anything funny and the girl gets it. I ain't got nothing to lose now.'

'Except perhaps your life, scumbag,' growled a well-known voice from behind. Wild Bill had been following the fleeing brigand. Ben had forced himself to remain calmly taciturn on witnessing the gunfighter creeping up behind. Before Crabbe could react, Bill had laid the barrel across his head. It was a brutal hit that knocked the felon to the ground. And there he stayed.

Bill was all set to drill him on the spot, but Ben stayed his hand. 'Reckon there's been enough blood-shed for one day, don't you agree, Bill?' Effy ran across to her beau, flinging her arms around him and held on tight as if her very survival depended on the steadfast maturity of this young lawman.

The renowned gunfighter kept his gun poised ready to deliver the killing shot, his deadpan look giving nothing away. Then he slowly relaxed, easing back the hammer and slotting the gun back into his waistband. 'You could be right there, young fella, but you make sure this guy don't slip through the net. His kind is more slippery than a wriggling eel.'

'We sure won't be allowing Mister Crabbe to escape the full rigour of the law, sir.' Along with the rest of the hidden audience, Mayor Scheffler had appeared once the danger was past. He now took control of the situation, gesturing for a couple of bystanders to carry the unconscious felon down to the hoosegow. No mention was made of the marshal overstepping his authority. 'The town sure does appreciate you helping our marshal out in his hour of need. There'll be a handsome reward coming for delivering up these outlaws.'

But Ben was done with law enforcement. All he wanted now was to settle down with the girl he loved and live a long life untroubled by a gunslinging rep-utation, and that could not happen around here. He tore off the tin star and handed it to the startled offi-cial.

'Me and my affianced intend moving far away from Sundance.' His eye met those of Estelle Wilmott, hoping that she felt the same. 'We want to grow oranges in California and spend the rest of our time raising a family. That right, Effy?'

Her adoring look supplied the affirmative answer. And with a dreamy smile embellishing her endearing features, she then planted a juicy kiss on her betrothed's lips to cement the union, much to the obvious delight of the gathered onlookers.